LIKE A SILVER BELL

A PORT WILLIS ROMANCE

LINDSAY HARREL

*To every woman who has ever felt less than, unworthy,
and unloved—you are not alone.*

CHAPTER 1

S ome said the devil was in the details.

But to Kara Elise Gentry, the details were the only thing that kept her sane—that kept her from thinking about the actual devil she had to face later tonight.

Kara clicked on her computer screen to bring up the flight schedule for tomorrow and breathed a sigh of relief that she and her traveling companions hadn't been unknowingly bumped to a later flight. With the time change from Boston to England, they were already losing five hours that could be used to work on the fundraiser. And with eleven hours of travel—

"Knock knock." Sarah Bentley-Hammett stuck her head into Kara's doorway. Today, the stylish CEO of New Dawn Women's Council—a nonprofit that provided free legal counsel to survivors of domestic violence during divorce and custody proceedings—wore low-slung heels and a blue dress that hugged her slightly rounded belly. Her red hair was pulled back in a loose bun at the nape of her neck. "You heading out soon?"

Kara pressed her hands down her green blouse, smoothing out an imaginary wrinkle. "Yes, I was just finishing up some last-minute prep for our trip."

A smile quirked her boss's lips. "Have I told you lately how amazing you are?"

Because there wasn't room in Kara's tiny office for more than a desk, chair, and filing cabinet, Sarah leaned against the doorway. But what the office lacked in size it made up for with an amazing view of downtown Boston out Kara's window that, at the moment, showcased the darkening sky and swirling snow of a December late afternoon.

Blushing, Kara pushed a strand of brown hair behind her ear. "Thank you." After a decade of being berated by Jeff, it was still difficult to accept compliments, but Kara's therapist reminded her often how important it was to try. Just try. "While I have you, can I get your thoughts on the final dinner menu for the ball?"

The upcoming fundraiser, which was the official launching point of New Dawn's London branch, consisted of a three-night stay at a historic manor in Cornwall and would culminate in a winter ball.

Sarah—who was still a born-and-bred member of Boston elite despite her marriage to a middle-class British photographer—and a few of her friends had leveraged their overseas contacts, and the fundraiser had sold out in days.

Now, it was up to Kara, New Dawn's special events coordinator, to make the whole affair a raging success.

Sarah swiped her hand through the air. "You don't need my input, Kara. How many fundraisers and charity events have you put together over the years? You've got this."

It was true. In her former role as the wife of Jeff Gentry, the CEO of Gentry Pharmaceuticals and all-around Boston golden boy, she'd hosted her fair share of events.

But it didn't matter how many events she had under her belt. This one mattered more than all of them combined, because she simply couldn't fail New Dawn. She *wouldn't*. The organization—and Sarah and Melissa, the wonderful ladies in charge—had not only rescued Kara from her ex-husband's clutches three years ago, but they'd also been kind enough to give her a job afterward. A job she'd so desperately needed.

Sure, Jeff had been forced to pay alimony in the divorce, but Kara refused to touch any of that man's money ever again. Every penny she received from him automatically went into Rose's college account.

Kara would prove to him—to everyone—that she could stand on her own two feet. It was what she should have been doing all along, really. If only she'd listened to her mother all of those years ago …

"I just want everything to go well." Kara fidgeted in her chair, her eyes flitting to the clock above the door. Time to go. "Never mind. The menu is fine, I'm sure." Well, not *sure*, but she didn't want to give her boss any reason to doubt her efforts.

"I sneaked a peek earlier, and it's not just fine. It sounds divine. Baby boy and I are more than excited to try the spiced Victoria sponge cake." Laugh lines creased the corners of Sarah's bright blue eyes. "Not that I need any more desserts. My belly is already humongous."

"It is not." Kara shut the lid of her laptop, unplugged it, and shoved it into her bag. "It's adorable." Sarah was five months along but looked more like two. "I wish I'd been that cute when I was pregnant with Rose."

Instead, Jeff had made sure Kara knew what a fat cow she'd become. At least he'd held off on hitting her for those nine months, though. Hadn't wanted to damage his "heir," after all.

Stop thinking about him. Kara hated that even now, there were times he and his words still got a hold of her. It had taken several years of therapy to become the functioning adult she was today, and she would not give him any more power than he'd already wielded in their seven-year marriage.

She and Sarah chatted for a few more minutes about the details of tomorrow, then Kara waved goodbye and started the forty-five-minute trek toward home. And despite the Christmas music she cranked in her twelve-year-old Corolla—a far cry from the brand-new Porsche she used to drive—she couldn't stop her mind from wandering to the task ahead of her.

The one that always made her sick to her stomach.

Maybe she'd get lucky and Jeff's housekeeper would answer the door instead. But probably not. Jeff knew how his presence grated on Kara. Even though he didn't control her like he once had, he still derived sick pleasure from her pain.

And nothing was going to be more painful than dropping Rose off for ten days with the monster who had made Kara's last ten years a living nightmare.

But rules were rules, and the judge had been clear —Kara had custody during the week, Jeff got Rose every other weekend, and the holidays were split fifty-fifty. Because Kara was going to be out of town for work, Jeff had agreed to take his holiday time with their daughter from December tenth through the twentieth, and then again for a few days at New Year's.

If only the judge had believed Kara about the abuse, she might have Rose full-time. But Kara's one comfort was that Jeff had never lifted a finger to harm his daughter. For all of his faults, he really did seem to love her—or at least, recognize that she was something special. And Kara made sure to take Rose to counseling regularly, on high alert for any abuse that might be occurring.

When Kara pulled into the driveway of Cindy and Travis's tiny three-bedroom craftsman, she inhaled deeply, determined her daughter would not sense her tension. Easing from the car, she tugged her coat closed to protect herself from the light snow flurries as she rushed to the front door.

"Hello," she called as she entered the place she and Rose had called home for the past three years. The vintage-decorated Christmas tree in the corner of the living room added a warm glow to the house, as did the tantalizing smell of cookies.

Kara hung her coat and purse on the entry-way rack and headed for the kitchen, where two voices sang along to "Rudolph the Red-Nosed Reindeer."

She stopped at the sight of her older sister and seven-year-old Rose belting into used egg beaters, their holiday spirit in full swing. Rose's wispy blonde hair was pulled back into a messy ponytail, and flour dusted the navy blue jumper and red long-sleeved polo she'd worn to school this morning. Jeff still insisted on her enrollment at the same prep school he'd attended as a child, and even though it now took her an extra thirty minutes to drive there every day—in the opposite direction from work—Kara had agreed.

Whenever possible, she tried not to violate the judge's custody order for "no unreasonable request" to be denied. Besides, the choice of school was not a hill she was willing to die on, especially when it was a good school and Jeff paid for it.

Rose's eyes widened when she caught sight of Kara. "Mommy!" She hopped down from her stool at the counter and raced to Kara, flinging herself into her arms. Kara leaned down and breathed in the warm scent of her daughter's skin—crayons and cinnamon.

"Hi, sweet pea." Kara pulled back and smoothed some flour off of Rose's smiling cheeks. "Smells delicious in here."

"Aunt Cindy said we should make some cookies for you to take to England." Rose's smile faltered for a minute as she tilted her head. "Do you really have to go?"

They'd been over this a thousand times already. As much as Kara loved the idea of a trip overseas in theory, it would hardly be all fun and games. "I'm afraid I do."

"Why can't I come?"

Kara caught Cindy's eye before her sister swiveled to place a cookie sheet in the oven and set the timer. Then she looked back at Rose. "I wish I could take you, but I'll be working the whole time. Plus, you've got another week of school, silly." She swallowed hard and forced a smile. "And your daddy is looking forward to spending time with you."

Rose's face brightened as she turned and skipped back to the counter, remounting her stool. "Maybe he'll take me to the movies. Regina doesn't like the movies, but I love them. So maybe."

Regina, Jeff's twenty-something girlfriend, didn't like a lot of things—including children, from what Kara could tell. More than once, Rose had come home telling Kara about something cruel the woman had said in passing. Thankfully, her daughter didn't seem to understand the slights.

Kara had complained to Jeff, but he'd only said she was exaggerating … and was she sure she wasn't jealous?

Striding to the counter, Kara shook out her hands. "Give me something to do. Got any cookie dough that needs pounding?"

Cindy's eyebrows lifted behind her wire-rimmed glasses as she slid a tray of cookies in front of Rose. "Not at the moment, but you can decorate these with Rose if you'd like."

"Perfect."

For the next half hour, Kara and her daughter sang along with silly Christmas songs and iced cookies, licking the red and green frosting from their fingers while Cindy stuck a casserole in the oven for dinner.

When a slew of messy treats dotted the counter and the smell of baked cheese and chicken filled the air, Kara glanced at the clock and held back a sigh. "Almost time to go, sweet pea. Is everything packed that you want to take to Daddy's?"

"Oh! There are a few things I forgot."

"Why don't you clean up and get those into your suitcase, okay? Then we'll eat a quick dinner and get going."

"Okay!" Rose hopped down and raced out of the kitchen.

"It's going to be so quiet around here with her at Jeff's and you gone." Cindy used a thick chef's knife to slice a tomato for the side salad. She was still dressed in simple slacks, a cozy sweater, and flats, her gray-streaked brown hair pulled back into a low ponytail—the perfect attire for an elementary school librarian.

Kara made her way to the sink and squirted soap in her hands, lathering it up until she could see her reflection in a few of the bubbles. "It'll be a welcome respite, I'm sure. When do Sam and Charlie get here?" Cindy was nine years older than Kara's thirty-eight years, and her two sons were currently away at college.

"Next Thursday." The sound of the knife hitting

the cutting board filled the modest kitchen. "It'll be nice to have us all together under one roof."

"I still feel bad for stealing their rooms." Kara washed the bubbles off her hands and down the drain, then dried off with the dish towel hanging from the oven handle. "Hopefully we'll be out of your hair soon. I've almost got the down payment for a house saved."

Okay, fine. She technically had enough as of last week. But saving even more couldn't be a bad thing, could it?

Her sister looked up, her gaze narrowed. "You are not in my hair."

"I know, I know."

"But ..."

Here it came. The big sister tone that Kara was oh so familiar with. But she couldn't blame Cindy.

"I do think it will be a good step toward recovery for you, to get your own place. In fact"—*thwap, thwap,* went the knife—"I forwarded you a few listings I found around here. They look really cute and affordable."

"I'll take a look when I get back from England." Kara tried to infuse enthusiasm into her voice. She *did* want to move out. Truly.

But what if ...

"I know you're worried about the nightmares scaring Rose, but you don't have them as frequently now."

Kara leaned against the counter. "You're right. Still …"

Cindy set down the knife and approached Kara, pulling her into a swift hug. "You know you'll always have a place here with me. I'm sorry if I'm being pushy. Just think about it, all right? For you. For Rose."

"I already told you that I'm going to do it." Because Kara would do anything to provide the most stable existence possible for her daughter. If only she could get past the paralyzing fear of being on her own. What if she failed her daughter … and herself … again? "It's just taking me a little longer than I'd hoped."

"I know, Sis." A pause. "Hey, so, how are you feeling about your trip? I know you'll be working, but I hope you at least try to enjoy your time overseas." Letting go, Cindy went back to her cutting board and placed the tomato into a bowl. "It'll be like a vacation. I mean, you'll be staying at a mansion, for goodness' sake."

Kara wandered to the counter and plucked out a juicy square of tomato. "Right. A vacation. What's that again?" She popped the piece into her mouth and chewed. Sweetness exploded on her tongue. Mmm. It was nice for food to have flavor again. She'd spent so much of her life in recent years fearful, depressed, that it had been hard to take pleasure in even the smallest things.

But she was making strides forward. Just not as quickly as she'd sometimes like.

Cindy hip bumped her sister out of the way and grabbed plates from the cupboard. "You should find out. Too bad you can't stay longer."

"There's no way I'm missing Christmas with Rose."

"Of course not." Cindy's mouth moved side to side as she snagged the stack of plates and placed them on the placemats at the eat-in table. "I just wish there was a way to get her to England once her time with Jeff is over."

Kara plucked a handful of cutlery from the silverware drawer and brought them to the table. "I'd never let her fly alone." But the idea of getting away for Christmas did sound lovely.

"I don't blame you." Without asking, Cindy took a few of the forks out of Kara's hands and placed them next to the plates. Once a big sister, always a big sister. "So …" She glanced up at Kara, eyebrow lifted.

"So, what?

"Will there be any handsome, single men at this event—in particular, the ball?"

"Stop." Kara snatched a dish towel off the counter and flicked it at Cindy, who laughed and dodged out of the way. "I'm going there to work, not to fall in love."

"Eh, semantics." Cindy snapped her fingers.

"What about that one man I met at the Christmas function last year? Winston something?"

"Warren? Warren Kensington?"

"Yes! Him. Will he be there? He's a cutie. Is he single?"

Kara's cheeks burned at the mention of the president of New Dawn's board of directors—because yes, she couldn't deny the guy was handsome with his broad shoulders, perfectly styled brown hair, and thick-framed glasses that reflected kind eyes behind them.

Or what seemed like kind eyes.

But Jeff's had seemed kind to her too, once upon a time.

She shook her head. "No."

"No, he won't be there? Or no, he's not cute? Or no, he's not single?" Cindy wagged her eyebrows as she set three wine glasses on the table, along with a milk cup for Rose.

"That's not—" Kara rolled her eyes and marched forward to grab the wine off the counter before Cindy could. She uncorked the bottle like a pro and began filling the glasses with the Chenin Blanc. "Yes, he will be there. The international board is taking the opportunity to have a meeting. And fine, he's attractive. I don't know if he's single, but I haven't heard of him dating anyone." She took a deep breath. "But Cin, he's also rich."

Cindy placed her hand over her mouth and

gasped—in an extremely exaggerated way that Kara did not appreciate. "No! Not that! Oh, cross him off the potential husband list right away then."

Pressing her lips together, Kara concentrated on not spilling a drop of the wine. "Even if I was going to let a new man into my life—and that's a big *if*—it wouldn't be a wealthy man. You know as well as I do what Tom did to Mom. I thought she was making it all up for attention. Or exaggerating at the very least."

"You can't trust a rich man, Kara. They'll take all your dreams and crush them. You've got to make sure you can stand on your own two feet."

And Kara had said the most horrific things in reply.

Now it was too late to apologize—her mother had died in a car accident a few years after their argument. "And then I went and did the very opposite of what she said. I married Jeff, a man ten times worse than Tom."

Ten times richer, too.

Not only had Jeff been abusive scum, but he was a liar to boot. All those nights he was gone, and she'd trusted that he was at work like he said … but then, when she'd started to wonder and asked him, he'd replied with his classic line: *"It's nothing you need to worry about."* Then he'd hit her for questioning his loyalty, even though her instincts had been correct.

Regina—and others like her—had been the real reason Jeff hadn't been warming his side of the bed.

"Kara."

She turned away from her sister and recorked the bottle. "I know what you're going to say, but it's no use. I'm not interested in dating again, anyway. I have Rose to consider. I can't afford to …" Oh no, she was *not* going to cry over this. Again.

Would it be nice to have a co-parent? Yes, oh yes. But only if he was a good man, one who would look past her scars and see someone worth loving.

As far as she was concerned, a man like that couldn't possibly exist.

Definitely not someone like Warren Kensington, a premiere member of the East Coast Elite. Just because she'd never seen him *act* entitled didn't mean he wasn't, deep down.

Cindy snagged her elbow and turned Kara gently toward her again. "Sis, I know you've walked a hard road. I've watched you take step after difficult step toward a brighter future. You are the bravest person I know." Her eyes radiated concern and unconditional love. "But you have to start trusting again."

"I do. I trust you." Kara wouldn't have survived the last few years without her sister, and she owed her everything. "And I trust Sarah and Melissa."

"That's not what I meant." Cindy tilted her head. "Someday, you're going to have to learn to trust men again."

Kara's eyes burned, and frowning, she bit the inside of her cheek. "Maybe."

But probably not. Because unless she could guarantee that she would never be lied to, betrayed—abused—again, she wouldn't allow a man into their lives.

And life just didn't come with those kinds of guarantees.

The next hour flew by until Kara loaded Rose and her stuff up into her car and started toward Jeff's historic home in Beacon Hill—the home where Kara had once lived in the lap of luxury.

But luxury was only skin deep, a fact of which she was now all too aware.

Rose chattered from the back seat, and Kara did her best to engage with her daughter—to keep her mind off of the reality of what she was about to do.

Maybe she'd been wrong. Maybe she *could* take Rose with her. Perhaps she could hire a sitter during the day while she worked. Rose would surely love to see the tiny Cornish village of Port Willis, all lit up for Christmas. And the gardens at the manor where they were holding the fundraiser were supposed to be some of the finest in the whole country. Rose could look at flowers for hours on end …

But no. Jeff would never allow it. And there would be too many details to work out in too short a time. Kara would just have to live with her decision and pray she'd made the right one.

Not that praying had done her much good over the years. Every time Jeff had lifted a fist, Kara would pray for him to stop.

He never had.

That's when Kara had known—she was the only one who could get herself out of the mess she'd somehow found herself in. Yes, others had been willing to help, but she'd had to be the one to take that first step toward being a survivor and not a victim.

And every day afterward, she had to keep stepping. Keep trudging.

For Rose.

Kara gripped the steering wheel harder and refocused on what her daughter was saying—something about the project she'd made in art class.

All too soon, they arrived at their destination.

As Kara and Rose got out of the car, Kara couldn't help the pinch in her chest that came every time she took in the beautiful home where she'd lived during her marriage to Jeff. The brick exterior had been restored, as had much of the inside, and there was a wide portico with columns flanking the doorway. An endless number of windows gave off a feeling of grandeur, of openness to passersby.

In reality, the place had been a prison.

Thankfully, Rose didn't seem to agree. She skipped right up the walkway and rang the doorbell. Even from out here, Kara could hear the ominous sound vibrating throughout the high-ceilinged entry. The wind whipped at the bottom of the black coat she'd found a few winters ago at Goodwill. It wasn't Gucci, but it kept her warmer than many coats she'd had as a child in a single-parent home—before her stepdad had swept into their lives and dropped them into a shiny new world.

Her spine stiffened as the large oak door creaked open slowly, every second adding to her rising anxiety.

Jeff stood on the other side. Her ex-husband still looked every inch the tall, chiseled forty-five-year-old man who commanded boardrooms and charmed everyone.

And he was still the man who haunted her nightmares.

"Daddy!" Rose flew into his arms, and Jeff took his eyes off of Kara for a moment to hug and kiss their daughter.

He pulled away and patted her cheek. "Doris has some cake waiting for you in the kitchen. Go put your things in your room first while I talk to your mom."

"Okay." Rose turned to Kara and gave her another hug that twisted Kara's gut. "See you soon, Mommy!" Then she skipped away down the hallway toward the staircase that led to her bedroom upstairs.

An awkward silence followed.

"So." Oh, wonderful. Of course her voice would choose this moment to crack. She didn't want Jeff to think his presence still had an effect on her whatsoever—even though it did. She cleared her throat. "I'll pick her up Monday the twentieth at seven in the evening as discussed."

"Hello, Elise." Jeff stuck his hands into the pockets of his slacks and leaned against his doorway, his figure backlit with the brilliance of the chandelier that they'd chosen together in the foyer. "It's nice to see you too."

She bit the inside of her cheek. "I've told you, it's Kara now. Again." She'd only gone by her middle name in the first place because Jeff liked it better. Said it sounded more distinguished, a better fit for the wife of a CEO. But she'd never felt like Elise. Elise was her great-aunt namesake who smelled like a strange mixture of fresh-cut grass and peppermint.

Returning to "Kara" had been her first step toward throwing off the proverbial shackles Jeff had placed around her wrists.

"Of course." Running his hand through his full head of black hair, Jeff flashed her that wolf-like grin she had once-upon-a-time found so irresistible. "Listen, about the twentieth …"

Something about his tone caused a jolt to her nervous system. "What?" Kara burrowed deeper into her coat.

"Forgive me. You look cold. Would you like to come in?" He stepped back and gestured toward the tiled entryway, where a sunburst pattern decorated the flooring. "Regina's not here right now. We could get drinks in my office. Catch up." He paused. "Revel in each other's company like old times."

Then he had the audacity to wink.

Kara had never been violent a day in her life, and yet, right now—with his dirty insinuations—she had the strongest urge to punch her ex in the teeth. But knowing him, he was baiting her. And he'd take her to court for violence so quick, that she'd lose her custody of Rose completely.

The idea of *her* losing custody for hitting *him* was quite ironic. And yet, that was her life.

"Thanks for that *oh-so-tempting* offer, but no." She straightened her back and dropped her arms, proving to him that she didn't need his warmth. Not anymore. "Now, what about the twentieth?"

The pungent smell of his sandalwood cologne wafted between them, and triggered the strong desire to flee. But she stood her ground.

"Regina has her heart set on taking a cruise for Christmas. It leaves on December nineteenth and returns on the twenty-ninth."

"Oh." Was that all? "I'm sure Cindy would be happy to watch Rose for the last few days of my trip."

"That's not what I'm saying." Jeff raised his strong, dark brow. "I want to take Rose with us."

"But—"

"I don't think it's terribly *unreasonable* for her to spend a memorable cruise with me during the holidays, do you? In exchange, she can be with you for New Year's and the next big holiday when I'm supposed to have her. Sound good?"

Unreasonable. There was that word again—the one the judge had used to set a precedent. The constant threat to their somewhat amicable custody arrangement. The one Jeff liked to throw in her face far too often.

But to take away Christmas with her girl? It was going too far. "No."

He tilted his head. "Come on, Elise. I mean, *Kara.*" Anyone else hearing the words probably wouldn't notice the sarcastic undertones, but Kara certainly did. "Rose would love it. And it wouldn't be the same without her there."

"Can't you do it a different time?"

Anytime but Christmas. Christmas wasn't like other holidays. It was … different. Special.

Despite so many years with nothing under the tree, Kara's mother had made sure that Christmas was always memorable for her and Cindy. Window shopping in the snow, a fifty-cent hot chocolate at Bernadette's Diner, a large candy cane stick that lasted for weeks, watching *Miracle on 34th Street* on the tattered couch in their mobile home—it had been magical.

Because they'd been *together*.

"I'm afraid this is a once-in-a-lifetime cruise. I won't bore you with the details, but suffice it to say that it's very exclusive and very expensive. I know you're not used to that anymore, but I won't deny Rose just because you choose to dress like you live in a halfway house."

Kara's fingers curled at the patronization dripping from Jeff's words.

"Besides, this way you can stay in England even longer than planned and get an actual vacation out of it. I imagine England is quite enchanting at Christmastime."

It probably was—but not without Rose. Her daughter was the only thing in the world that mattered. Everything Kara did, she did for Rose.

That's why she was going overseas before Christmas in the first place—because work required it, and work meant a paycheck, and a paycheck meant their own home, and their own home meant stability.

Maybe she could sweet-talk him. The idea made her shudder, but she had to try. Kara put on a quiet, submissive tone. "Jeff…"

"I hate to do this, El—Kara—but I've got the judge on speed dial." He pulled out his phone and waved it in the air. "Maybe we should see what *he* thinks of your refusal. Whether he thinks it's reasonable."

Kara took a step backward, nearly stumbling off the porch stoop. How did he—? But of course he had the judge's number. *Of course* he was buddy-buddy with the guy. Probably played golf with him too. Maybe even had slipped him a bribe at some point.

It was the way of rich men to protect each other from every bad thing they deserved.

And Kara was just a mom trying to fight for her daughter. All she had was love and the backing of a few well-meaning family members and friends.

But none of those people was strong enough to win the war with Jeff completely. Sarah and her business partner, Melissa, had already fought hard to get Kara the current arrangement.

The last thing Kara wanted to do was bow to Jeff and his whims. But what choice did she have? One wrong maneuver and she just might lose Rose forever—New Dawn or no New Dawn.

She gave a clipped nod. "Fine. Take your cruise. But she calls me frequently. And I will get her on the thirtieth and not a day later."

"Of course, of course." Grinning, Jeff shoved his phone back into his pocket. "Thank you for being so accommodating."

As if I have a choice.

"Let me tell Rose what's going on."

"Ah, ah, ah." Jeff tsked. "This is my time now. I'll inform Rose about the change of plans."

She knew better than to argue or plead. But she wouldn't have him thinking she was a wilting flower. Not anymore. Kara narrowed her eyes. "You'd better not spin it as me abandoning her for work."

"I hadn't thought of that ..." Jeff rubbed his chin, grinning.

Holding back a growl, she longed to say just the right thing to put him in his place. But nothing would because he belonged in—

Calm down, Kara. This is what he wants. You, angry. He's trying to control your emotions again.

"I'll be calling your phone to speak with her tomorrow. She'd better be available." Kara turned on her heel and walked away from him, fighting the falling tears at the prospect of Christmas without her baby.

What a dreary holiday this was turning out to be. And yet, somehow, she had to make it magical for a hundred-plus donors who were about to travel to Port Willis expecting a grand time.

Okay, then. Kara stomped through the snow, each step more determined than the last.

She would throw every ounce of energy into doing what she did best—organizing, planning, and making sure everyone else was happy.

CHAPTER 3

*J*eff might be a lying, abusive jerk, but he was right about one thing—England *was* enchanting at Christmastime.

Kara turned slowly, taking it all in. From her spot, where the Port Willis harbor met the end of High Street, she could see a good chunk of the Cornish village. Dinghies and other small fishing craft bobbed in the waves that were gentled by the rocky quay extending parallel to the land. Adorable wooden storefronts painted in a variety of pastels lined the cobblestone street, piping smoke into Sunday's early evening sky.

She, Sarah, and Sarah's husband, Michael—New Dawn's photographer—had only been in town a few hours, after their long trek had landed them finally at Cornwall Airport Newquay. There, Sarah's in-laws had picked them up and dropped Kara's luggage by Rebecca's, an adorable bed and breakfast taking up residence next to a charming bookstore and bakery combo.

That was the whole town—adorable. And so different from the hustle and bustle and smog of Boston.

Kara couldn't wait to see the manor where the fundraiser would take place. It was several miles outside of town, but if it was anything like the village itself, the pictures wouldn't do it justice.

After the stop at the B&B, Michael's parents had insisted Kara join them for a late lunch at their restaurant, the Village Pub, where she'd had her fill of delicious roasted chicken stew and homemade bread. Sarah's younger sister and brother-in-law, Ginny and Steven Applegate, had joined them, as had Michael's sister and her young family.

It had been a loud, raucous affair, but Kara was glad for some quiet just now.

Though she'd hated to admit how tired she was—lack of sleep plus jet lag would do that to a person—the fact that Kara had nearly fallen asleep in her meal had been a fairly good indicator. A walk would be just what she needed to unwind from the lengthy travel and keep her awake until evening.

She started the jaunt back toward the bed and breakfast, anxious to change into loungewear and curl up with a mug of hot chocolate and a good book. Most of the shops—from an antique store to a grocer to a few restaurants—appeared to be closed. Sarah had mentioned something about Sundays being big family days here. The thought pierced Kara's chest. Her own family was so far away.

Reaching into her purse, she pulled out her phone and dialed Jeff's number for the first of her daily chats with Rose. The phone rang and rang before rolling over to voicemail, and her chest tightened even more. Jeff had better not try to keep Rose from talking with her. They'd agreed.

Not that he kept his word all that often. But still. Kara would go full mama bear on him if he tried to withhold her daughter.

She left Rose a quick, peppy voicemail asking her to call back soon and hung up just as she passed a small park that sat on the bluffs overlooking the ocean. "Wow."

Her feet tugged her forward. On one end of the park was a small playground where a handful of children played. Kara listened to the sound of young laughter, wishing Rose's was among them. What was her daughter doing right now? Was Jeff taking good care of her, or was she hanging out in her room or on the iPad he'd insisted on getting for her even though Kara disapproved?

Shaking free of the thoughts, Kara moved toward a gazebo at the opposite end of the park. Beside it stood a Christmas tree that must have been fifteen or maybe even twenty feet tall. It was decorated with red and silver bulbs and strand after strand of darkened lights. The gazebo roof had also been strung with lights. She imagined it all lit up against the sky—gorgeous, especially if the stars shone out here with any amount of brightness. The clouds would need to clear away first, though.

A sudden gust of wind whipped Kara's hair back from her face and she hurried toward the gazebo, where a ring of wooden benches would allow her to sit in shelter and enjoy the scenery.

She didn't notice someone already sat there until she was nearly inside.

Him.

Kara halted. Oh no. She could almost hear Cindy cackling with glee from across the pond.

But maybe if she backed away slowly, he wouldn't notice her.

No such luck.

The man glanced up from his phone and blinked a few times. "Kara?"

"H-hi, Warren." She swallowed, her throat suddenly dry. "Good to see you."

Warren tucked away his phone and stood. "You too." He wore jeans that likely cost more than she made in a month, a fashionable black trench coat—probably Burberry—and a purple woven scarf that looked both stylish and functional. Though Kara wasn't petite by any means, his solid presence made her feel short. "Did you just get into town?"

She straightened her spine, hoping to appear taller than she was. Not that it mattered what he thought. "Yes, a few hours ago. I'm staying at a bed and breakfast not far from here and thought a walk sounded nice."

Sarah and Michael were bunking with Ginny and Steven, who had also invited Kara along—but she preferred to have her own place to retreat to. Plus, she'd be in and out so much with preparing for the fundraiser and didn't want to disturb anyone.

"Rebecca's? Me too." A smile lit Warren's face. Though he was normally clean-shaven, today a dusting of dark stubble covered his sculpted jaw, lending him a rather rugged appeal.

And why exactly are you noticing that?

Kara bit the inside of her cheek. "Small world."

He chuckled. "Not as small as you'd think. I'm pretty sure this town only has a few places to stay."

"Right." Taking a step backward, Kara forced a smile. "Well, I'd better be getting back there. Work is calling my name."

"I'll join you if you don't mind. I've got hundreds of emails to comb through myself." In addition to heading up New Dawn's board, he was in charge of the Boston branch of his family's New York-based corporation, which specialized in everything from technology to pharmaceuticals.

Warren stepped forward, and Kara caught a whiff

of mandarin orange, black pepper, and lavender. It sent a shiver through her.

Goodness. For the scent of mere cologne to have such an effect on her, she really *was* tired—either that or Cindy's words from two days ago had unfortunately embedded themselves in her brain.

Well, her brain had better get the memo that her heart was trying to send it.

No romance.

Especially not with him.

"Sure. I guess if we're both headed that way." It wasn't as if walking with him signified anything. Besides, he was on the board of directors, which kind of indirectly meant he was one of her bosses, right? She should be polite to her boss.

Kara headed back toward the street.

Following along, Warren inhaled a deep breath and stuck his hands inside the pockets of his coat. "It's nice to be back here."

"You've been to Port Willis before?"

"Once. Three years ago." He glanced at her. "It was actually on that trip that I decided to become part of what New Dawn was doing."

Three years … right about the time she'd decided to leave Jeff.

"Has the town changed much?" Because the last three years had changed everything for her.

"Not really. I think that's what I love about this place—so classically charming, like something out of a painting or kids' storybook. It's why I suggested we hold the fundraiser here instead of London."

As they crossed the street, an old metal lamppost flickered on. Dusk had arrived.

Kara lifted an eyebrow. "That was your idea?" To be honest, when she'd first heard it, she'd thought it a bit of a risk. "How did you know donors would want to travel down here so close to the holidays?" Most of them were not only busy but also lived in London, a four- or five-hour drive from Cornwall.

He shrugged. "I just thought about my ideal holiday and figured others might feel the same way."

Well, that was a mysterious answer. "What's your ideal holiday?" She really didn't want to ask such personal details of him, but it would be good to understand the mindset of the guests who would be attending the fundraiser. After all, if their expectations weren't met, she wouldn't have done her job.

And they wouldn't be likely to donate again.

"Oh, nothing fancy—though I know the ball will be a hit." Warren stepped off the sidewalk onto the street so a family with a stroller could pass. He smiled and nodded a greeting at them before refocusing on Kara. "Mostly, just time away from the craziness of work, a place where I can breathe, where normal life seems a world away."

"You can't get much farther from the norm than here, I suppose." She followed him as he continued around a bend in the road. The bed and breakfast loomed in the distance. "What about planned activities? I have some options for people—daytime sightseeing, tours about the estate grounds, and some nighttime activities in town and at the manor—but I thought most might want to plan their own excursions." She hoped she was right in that regard.

"That sounds great. Our lives are so over-planned already, our calendars so crowded, that I think guests might appreciate some downtime." He chuckled. "Although some might not know what to do with themselves."

"True." She tilted her head, curious about something. "Pardon me for asking, but is that why you're here so much earlier than the other board members?" As far as she knew, they weren't set to arrive until the day before the other donor guests did on Thursday.

Warren nodded. "Sarah invited me to come out early and spend some time with them." He reached for the handle of Rebecca's front door. "Over the last several years, I've become closer with her and Michael than my own family."

Huh. And why was that?

But no. She closed her lips before she could ask the question. She didn't need to know anything more than necessary about this man—however pleasant he was being in this moment.

As he opened the door, a rush of warm air met Kara's cheeks. She inhaled the lovely scent of spiced cake and apple cider, which sat on the sidebar of the smallish dining room to the right of the entryway. A petite woman with dirty blonde hair stood behind a wooden desk—Rebecca Trengrouse, the owner. She gave a gruff wave to Kara and Warren before turning back to her computer screen.

It had been a while since Kara had stayed at a bed and breakfast—the last one had been in the Poconos for her and Jeff's third anniversary—and the first time she'd been at one by herself. But one glance at the cozy living room warmed by a stone fireplace that was flanked by bookcases and an undecorated Christmas tree, and Kara knew she'd found a home away from home.

She'd stay here every night of her trip if she could, but she needed to be on hand at the estate come Thursday and until she flew out next Sunday. Unless she decided to stay longer, like Cindy had suggested when Kara had told her about the change of Christmas plans. Hmm.

Either way, for now, she'd enjoy the peace. The quiet. The warmth.

Kara let loose a contented sigh.

"It's quite charming, isn't it?"

Her hand flew to her chest. Right. Warren was still with her, wasn't he?

"Yes." She grimaced at the sudden coolness in her voice. "I guess I'll see you around."

"It'll be hard not to. I think we're the only guests staying here this week."

Her breathing ratcheted up a notch. "What?"

That couldn't be right. Surely more would be coming in at some point. She'd have to check with Rebecca. Otherwise, how was she supposed to avoid Warren? Kara already didn't like her body's response to him. And with the absence of Rose and the stress of pulling off this event, her mind was in a fragile place.

She could not afford any distractions—even one so handsome as Warren Kensington.

As quick as St. Nick in that Christmas Eve poem her mom had read to her and Cindy as kids, the peace Kara had sensed in this place flew out the charming little B&B window.

CHAPTER 4

She'd slept surprisingly well. No nightmares as far as she could remember.

Hopefully today's mission—running through details with the fundraiser venue's events coordinator—wouldn't be a nightmare either.

Kara's stomach rumbled as she made her way down the stairs to breakfast. The aroma of sausages drifted up the staircase from the dining room, where she found Rebecca reading a newspaper and eating breakfast at the twelve-person oak table.

The woman, who must have been about Kara's age, glanced up and set her paper aside. "Morning." Her voice wasn't exactly chipper, but not unfriendly either.

"Good morning." Kara glanced between Rebecca and the covered dishes on the sidebar. She didn't see any coffee—and that was a necessity. "Could you please direct me to wherever the drinks are?"

"I've only got tea, juice, and water." The owner fluttered her hand. "If you're looking for that dark, terrible drink that you Americans enjoy, you'll have to go a few doors down to Ginny's bakery. I refuse to make it." Rebecca made a face. "Can't stand the stuff or the smell."

Kara didn't know what to make of this B&B owner who wouldn't cater to her guests, but something about the small woman's chin tilted in challenge—as if she was used to the whole world being against her, used to having to fight for what she wanted—instantly made her feel like a kindred spirit.

She smiled. "Tea is fine, then."

Standing, Rebecca grunted her approval. "Earl Grey or English breakfast?"

"Surprise me."

After staring at Kara for a moment, she nodded and flounced from the room. Kara took the opportunity to surreptitiously glance about the room. No Warren in sight. Perhaps he'd already left for the day, or maybe he was using this opportunity to sleep in. Whatever the case, hopefully she could make it through breakfast without a forced interaction.

Not very professional of her, but there it was.

She walked to the sidebar and lifted the lid off the first platter to reveal sausage links and scrambled eggs. After placing a spoonful of eggs and two links on a china plate, she moved onto the bowl of pears and snatched one out, ignoring the stack of delicious-looking pastries before heading back to the table. Experience told her that her dress for the ball wouldn't fit if she overindulged in the days leading up to the event.

Just then, Rebecca returned carrying a steaming cup of tea on a saucer. She plopped it in front of Kara and pushed a small creamer toward her. "It's best with a spot of milk."

"Thank you." Kara lifted the porcelain container and poured in a dash of the liquid, stirring it with the tiny spoon set on the saucer. "How long have you owned this bed and breakfast?"

Picking up her fork, Rebecca pushed the remainder of her eggs around her plate. "Two years now. My dad owned the bakery in town—Trengrouse Bakery, not the one Ginny runs—since before I was born, but he closed up shop after Ginny opened hers. He was ready to retire, you see." She stabbed the eggs. "It took time to make peace with that, but now Ginny and I get on just fine. Not sure her sister holds much affection for me, though."

"Sarah?" Kara's boss could be tough if she needed to be, but she was all softness and goodness as far as Kara could tell. Maybe that was a story for another time, though. She took a sip of her tea, and hummed in pleasure at the notes of bergamot.

"Yep." Rebecca finally took a bite of her eggs. "Anyway, Dad was kind enough to give me my share of the proceeds as a sort of inheritance, so I bought this place. Used to be Loretta's, but Loretta wanted to retire, so I took it off her hands for a steal." She pointed to the doily-laced tablecloth. "Not exactly my style, but I don't have the funds to change out the decor just yet. Guests seem to like it all right, though, so no matter."

Kara lifted a sausage to her lips. "It's a lovely place, that's for sure. I can't wait to sit in that armchair over there and read by the fireplace." If she had any time to do so. She bit into the sausage and chewed, sighing at the burst of spicy flavor in her mouth.

"You won't have much competition for it. I have a whole party that's coming in this weekend—just in time for the forecasted snow—but no one during the week." Rebecca studied her like a mom watching a child for a reaction. "So it's just you and Tall, Dark, and Handsome for the next several days."

Focusing all her attention on her breakfast, Kara felt her cheeks go hot. So Warren had been correct. Well, that didn't matter. With how busy she was going to be, she'd hardly see him.

As if sensing her need for a change in subject—stat—the B&B's front door opened and in breezed a woman even shorter than Rebecca.

With blonde hair that came to her shoulders, a

bright orange puffy coat, and dangling neon green earrings, Joy Lincoln was a walking ad for confidence. "Hello!"

"Joy!" Smiling, Kara rose to greet her friend, whom she'd met only once in person but many times over video chat. "So good to see you again."

Joy yanked her into an enthusiastic hug. "Same to you." The forty-six-year-old had way more energy than most twenty-somethings Kara knew. She released Kara. "I'm so excited to show you Pendolphin House."

Joy, an American who had married a Brit she'd met while at a friend's wedding in Port Willis four years ago, was a women's therapist living in London. She believed in New Dawn's mission so much that she'd donated hours of her time to make the launch of the new branch a success. In fact, she'd been the one to scout the perfect location for the fundraiser and meet with vendors that Kara had chosen from afar.

Together, they'd make this fundraiser a success.

"And I can't wait to see it." Kara took a final sip of her tea. "Thank you for the lovely breakfast, Rebecca, but I've got to scoot. Should I take my dishes to the kitchen?"

Rebecca eyed Joy warily, but waved her hand at Kara. "No need. Go enjoy yourself."

Joy glanced at Kara, clear mirth in her eyes and a

twitch at her lips. "I'll go keep the car warm while you get your things."

"Thanks." Kara ran upstairs, threw on her jacket, and grabbed her purse from the adorable nightstand. She tossed on a black beanie for good measure. It didn't snow often or all that much in Cornwall, but her weather app had shown a dip in temperature for today.

Snatching her gloves, she turned and cruised out of her room—and right into a solid chest.

"Whoa." Strong arms held her steady, and the most glorious whiff of fresh, manly shampoo surrounded her. "Sorry. You all right?"

She jerked away from Warren, who very obviously had just come from the still-steamy bathroom across the hall. His normally gelled hair was damp, making it appear longer than normal, and he wore a simple white T-shirt and sweatpants. She would have expected him to wear slippers, but no—his feet were bare.

Something about seeing him so casual did things to her insides. Things she didn't like.

"Kara? Are you okay?" Warren's voice indicated his clear concern.

And now she was staring. "Oh. Yeah. I'm fine. Sorry for nearly running you down."

"No worries." He chuckled and ran a hand through his hair. She tried to ignore the way his bicep bulged with the motion. "Where are you off to in such a hurry this morning? Trying to beat me to the coffee?"

At that, she couldn't help but smile. This man, who was used to everyone catering to his every whim, was about to get the shock of his life. Kara leaned in like she had a secret. "Rebecca doesn't believe in coffee."

"What?"

She giggled—giggled!—at the incredulous look on his face. But it was too funny to suppress her laughter. "She said we had to go to Ginny's bakery if we want any."

"I guess you know where I'll be all day then."

Her nose scrunched. He hadn't reacted in the way she'd expected. If he'd been Jeff or anyone in his inner circle, Warren would have marched down the stairs and demanded Rebecca make him a batch of coffee on the double—because he was the guest, and the guest was always right. Always entitled. They were the ones with the money, after all.

But instead, he'd rolled with the punches and accepted Rebecca's little quirk—and hadn't even gotten upset about it.

What was Kara supposed to make of that?

Nothing. It doesn't matter. He doesn't mean anything to you, remember?

Right. Right!

"Okay, well, I've gotta go. I need to check out the venue and all that."

"That sounds much more fun than my activities for the day. I'm tempted to tag along."

"No!" She was already having trouble reminding herself that he wasn't someone she wanted to get close to. If she were forced to spend the whole day with him, it would be even harder. And she needed to focus today.

But oh man, if the crinkled corners of his eyes and frown were any indication, her outburst had clearly hurt his feelings. And he hadn't done anything to deserve that.

"Um, that is, you'd be bored. We've got a thousand details to still work out, and I know you're working today. And you have lunch with Sarah and Michael, right?" Hadn't he mentioned something about that? No? Maybe? "Anyway, I'd hate to keep you from ... whatever. Okay, bye."

She scrambled away before he could answer, mentally kicking herself for how she'd sounded.

Desperate.

Unconfident.

Weak.

Kara shook out her hands as she walked down the stairs and out the front door, calling goodbye to Rebecca and receiving another grunt in reply. Joy was waiting in a cute yellow Smart car and didn't look intimidated in the least to be driving on the "wrong" side of the road. Guess she'd had lots of practice over the last several years.

Climbing inside, Kara set her purse at her feet and buckled herself in. "This is cozy."

Joy lovingly pet the dashboard. "I love Rascal here."

"Rascal?" Kara couldn't help the laugh that exited her mouth as Joy pulled out of their spot and onto High Street. The Monday morning traffic was heavier than yesterday, but nothing compared with Boston.

"Yes, Rascal. Named after the beloved dog that brought Oliver and me together." Joy smiled as if lost in thought.

"Oh, I'm so sorry. When did he pass away?"

"Pass away?" Joy arched an eyebrow, then seemed to realize Kara's assumption. "Oh, he's still very much kicking. In fact, he rules the roost in our home. We've adopted five others since and he acts like a mama to them all."

"You have six dogs?" Kara settled into her seat and watched the scenery change out her window as they left Port Willis behind and headed for the open road. Dark clouds gathered on the horizon. Apparently they were in for a storm later today.

"Yes, and I'd get more if we had the space." Joy sighed. "I've tried convincing Oliver to move from our London flat to the country, but it's just not practical with our work situations. Maybe someday."

Oliver owned an accounting firm in the city, and Joy had started working part-time at a shelter for battered women. They'd moved to London full-time a year ago after Joy's mom had passed away from Alzheimer's. Her dad had decided to stay in Florida, except in the hot summers when he visited them for three or four months at a time.

The trees outside Kara's window swayed in the breeze and the countryside bluffs rolled past. Sheep grazed in a far-off meadow. If Rose had been here, she'd have begged to stop and pet them. Not that Kara would have allowed it—weren't sheep notoriously filthy?—but the thought made her miss her daughter something fierce. She'd never gotten ahold of Jeff last night and would have to find time tonight after Rose was done with school to call. Hopefully this time, he'd answer.

"We're actually about to enter Pendolphin land." Joy turned off the main road and pointed to a stone arch extending over the smaller road they were now on. "You probably remember this from the website, but it's one hundred acres and our guests will have access to the whole place, including the surrounding land."

"It's so beautiful." Trees and seasonal flowers dotted the green landscape. Kara remembered from the map that the estate backed a gorgeous cliffside view of the Atlantic. "Hopefully the snow doesn't keep them from enjoying the outdoors."

"Eh, the snow is usually just a dusting." Joy tapped the steering wheel to an imaginary tune.

"Not like the year Sophia got married, and Oliver and I were trapped in London together overnight in a freak snowstorm."

Whoa. "That sounds like quite a story."

Joy's tinkling laughter filled the vehicle. "Not as scandalous as it sounds, but yes. Quite a story indeed." She squinted ahead. "Look. There's the house."

Kara inhaled a sharp breath that got caught in her lungs at the sight before her. A three-story house that rivaled Pemberley in the *Pride & Prejudice* movies sat at the end of a long drive. Its facade was made of gray stone and colonnaded wings of brick, with an array of windows that must let in a lot of whatever light the country sun might afford. At least a half dozen chimneys topped the manor, showcasing the sheer volume of rooms that were visible just from the front. A series of stone steps descended from the large entryway into a graded walkway that led to the lush gardens.

"It's perfect."

"Isn't it?" Joy guided the car up the driveway and parked in a small lot off the side. "And I know you've talked with her a few times, but the coordinator, Meg, is wonderful. She's more than willing to answer any of our questions, and she's been very on the ball with everything I've asked of her so far."

Kara climbed from the vehicle. The air felt somehow crisper out here—probably something about the countryside. "She seems to be really accommodating and organized."

A few minutes later, when she met Meg for the first time in person, Kara found her first impression to be true. The woman gave them a tour of the house and grounds—all beautiful—and after that was complete, Meg handed Kara a copy of the detailed plan for the upcoming weekend.

Everything seemed to be perfectly in place. All signs pointed to the fact that Kara could relax a bit. That the fundraiser was going to go off without a hitch.

She was tempted to wonder what could go wrong. But that was a question no events coordinator should ever ask.

Besides, in her experience, it was just when life seemed grandest that it turned and slapped a person in the face.

❄

*K*ara probably should go to bed.

But the licking flames of the fire in the hearth were mesmerizing, especially when combined with the Christmas music lilting across the airwaves from Rebecca's radio up front. Add to that the hot cocoa in the mug currently clutched between Kara's hands, and her life was a gorgeous, pine-scented Christmas commercial.

And yet, she still couldn't fully relax.

Because despite the hours she'd spent this afternoon and evening poring over Meg's binder and finding no discrepancies with her well-crafted plan, Kara couldn't seem to quiet that pesky ball of worry in the pit of her stomach. Ultimately, if anything went wrong with this fundraiser event, it wouldn't be Meg's reputation and career on the line. It would be Kara's.

Not that Sarah would fire her, but Kara would never forgive herself if the fundraiser flopped.

Tomorrow, she'd head back to Pendolphin House to lead the decoration efforts. But tonight, there was nothing more to be done. She glanced at the clock—eight nineteen. Too late to do anything in town, since most of the shops closed before dinner this time of year. And much as she loved reading, her nerves were too shot to concentrate on anything.

Kara stood, stretched her back, and walked toward the front desk. Maybe talking to Rebecca would ease her tension. The woman had the uncanny ability to make her laugh.

But she wasn't at reception. Perhaps the kitchen …

As Kara swung through the door, she pulled up short at the sight of Rebecca and Warren rolling cookie dough. Warren's cheeks wore a five o'clock shadow and a few dots of flour, and he listened intently while Rebecca bossed him around. The innkeeper rolled her eyes at something Warren said, and he laughed despite her unsmiling demeanor.

This certainly wasn't a sight Kara had expected to see. First, a man like Warren baking, but also, the two of them … together. Could it be their host held some affection for the handsome VP?

Something twisted in Kara's gut at the thought.

Which was ridiculous. Surely Warren had women all over the globe constantly throwing themselves at him. Why should Kara care?

I don't.

Whatever was going on here though, she wasn't going to interrupt. Slowly, she backed out of the kitchen.

But just before she'd fully exited, Rebecca looked up. "Oh good. Are you done working?"

Warren's gaze connected with Kara's, and she hated the way her body responded to the pools of chocolate in his eyes—flushing warm and tingling all over.

She cleared her throat. "Yep. About to head to bed. Just wanted to say good night."

Rebecca shook her head. "Nope, you can't yet." She left her dough on the counter, turned to wash her hands in the sink, and dried them on her apron before turning back to Warren and blinking. "Well, come on. I need your help. Both of you." Then she sprung from the room.

Warren just stood there for a moment, hands still sunk into the dough. "She sure is … spirited."

"That's one word for it."

A smile touched the corners of his lips. "I guess we should follow her, huh?" He released the dough and cleaned off his hands.

Kara shrugged. "I suppose so."

Warren stepped toward her, but halted—almost like he'd thought better of crowding her. "Sorry." Then he gestured toward the door. "After you."

They left the kitchen, Warren behind her but not close. Why had he apologized? Was he just being thoughtful? Perhaps, given her past, he thought she'd be jumpy around men. And maybe at times she was. But while something about him set her on edge, it wasn't fear—not fear that he'd hurt her, anyway.

She hadn't felt zings of attraction like this since … well, since Jeff.

And *that's* what scared her.

When they emerged in the living room, Rebecca was nowhere to be found. "Hello?" Kara called.

"In here!" The muffled voice seemed to be coming from a hall closet sitting ajar on the other side of the room.

Kara and Warren made their way over and found Rebecca tugging on a large box, huffing like she had a house to blow down. The woman threw her hands on her hips. "Don't just stand there. Help me!"

Together, the three of them lifted the box and set

it down beside the Christmas tree as directed by Rebecca.

"What's inside?" Warren asked, massaging his chin.

Rebecca tugged a box cutter from the back pocket of her jeans like it was the most natural tool to carry around. "Your project for the evening." She sliced the tape and opened the box to reveal holiday ornaments of all shapes and sizes—from dainty bells and lace-encrusted balls to sparkling figurines and vintage-looking candy canes.

Kara pulled loose a tiny snow globe ornament with a bit of snow and a tree tucked inside a clear round shell. "What do you mean, our project?"

"For every group that comes to stay here, I un-decorate the tree and allow them to re-decorate it. It's a tradition Loretta started. And, I don't know, I liked the idea of a fresh start every week." She stared at Kara, her nose scrunched. Then she glanced at Warren, before returning her gaze to Kara. "Well, go on, then. Have at it."

Wait. Suddenly the fire felt warmer than before. "Aren't you going to help?"

"I've got cookies to bake. Besides, it's a tradition for the guests to enjoy. And since you two are my only guests at the moment…"

Kara felt Warren's eyes on her but couldn't bring herself to look. A few run-ins, that was one thing. But an entire evening, just the two of them, decorating the tree like they were in some cozy Hallmark movie?

Just … no. "Um, like I said, I was headed for bed."

Rebecca's eyes narrowed. "Fine, I'll make you coffee if you insist. But only so you can stay awake. Tomorrow, we return to tea and only tea." Her petite frame charged from the room once again. Did the woman ever slow down? She was like a train going full steam ahead at all times.

And right now, though she'd left the room, she was steamrolling Kara.

She leaned against the back of one of the winged chairs, digging her fingers into the *fleur-de-lis*-patterned fabric. How was she going to get out of this without being rude? "Warren …"

"It's okay." His voice was gentle as he knelt beside the box and began pulling ornaments from inside, arranging them along the stone base that stuck out from the fireplace. "I can do it myself."

There was something dejected in his tone—almost disappointed. No, that couldn't be right. Why would he care if she helped or not?

But before she could really examine his reaction further, her attention snagged on one of the ornaments he'd unearthed. Her breath caught and she surged forward. Kneeling beside Warren, she picked up the ornament and cradled it in her fingers. The tiny glass figurine depicted Santa on a rocking horse.

Her hands shook.

"Everything okay?"

"What?" She glanced up at him, blinked, then looked away again. "Oh, yeah. It's just … I got Rose this exact ornament for her first Christmas. It … it broke."

Or rather, two years later, while decorating their tree as a family—the one and only time they'd done so—Kara had said something careless and Jeff had thrown it at her face. It had fallen and shattered on their wooden floors. Then he'd made her walk barefoot across the broken glass to get the broom and clean it up.

Her heart ratcheted up at the memory.

"You must miss her a lot."

Warren's soft voice contrasted sharply with the remembrance, but it was enough to tug Kara away from that time. Enough to make her want to remake her memory of this ornament into something pleasant.

Surely she could spend one evening making a tree beautiful, even if it meant enduring an hour or two alone with Warren. It beat going back to her room and facing the quiet, which—after that terrifying flashback—was sure to be filled with screams of her past.

So, Kara stood, walked to the tree, and placed the Santa ornament on one of the branches. "I do miss her. Because of the time difference, finding the right time to connect the last few days has been difficult." In fact, she'd only managed to catch a five-minute call with Rose today because of homework and dinner plans that Jeff had made with his parents.

"What do you miss most?" Warren snagged a few ornaments and moved past Kara to hang them, unaware of how his casual question had stilled Kara in her tracks.

To be honest, every instinct in her body yelled at her to run up the stairs and not come back down until Warren Kensington was nowhere in sight.

But why? He'd only asked a simple question—one that actually showed he cared. That he was interested in her life, even if he was just making simple conversation for conversation's sake.

Was she so screwed up now that she was suspicious of every man's motives in asking about her life?

Or was it more?

Kara forced herself to take up another few ornaments and arrange them on the other side of the tree from where Warren stood fluffing a few branches. Inhaling a breath, she answered his question. "Everything. Her little girl smell. Her smile that can melt the heart of the Scroogiest Grinch. The sweet way she takes my cheeks between her hands and reminds me it's going to be okay."

She paused with an ornament mid-air, nearly choking on the last words as the memories surged fast and sure. "She's had to do that a lot over the last three years." Kara blinked away a few tears. Ugh. Why had she said that? The last thing she wanted to do was talk with Warren about what she'd been through.

All he needed to know was that she was capable of doing the job that the board—and Sarah—had hired her to do. So far, she'd proven her worth. That was all that mattered.

And yet, when the silence grew between them to an uncomfortable degree, she lifted her head to find him watching her. "I'm sorry, Kara."

She shrugged a shoulder. "It's fine. In the past. We're all good now." Turning, she swiped at her eyes before grabbing yet another ornament. "What about you? What are you missing this Christmas?"

Please, please, please let him take the hint. *Move on.*

After a moment, Warren ran a hand through his hair and studied the tree, frowning as he repositioned a few ornaments. "If I were a good son, I'd say my parents."

"I'm sure you're a good son." Shoot. Had that sounded flirty? Kara rushed on. "I mean, you're generally a good person, so …" Ugh, no. That was worse.

But it was true. Right?

Or was she just being fooled by a handsome face and rich exterior once more?

Then again, had Jeff ever been this … relaxed? This mellow? This easy to talk to? They'd only ever decorated the tree together the one time, and it was because Kara had begged.

No, looking back, all of her dates with Jeff revolved around public events—chances to show her off as a trophy of sorts. Expensive dinners out. The opera. Fundraisers that started at one thousand dollars a plate. They had never been the couple who sat on the couch after work watching television and eating takeout. He'd been too busy. Too self-absorbed to really see her and what she wanted.

And not that she was perfect, but Kara didn't care about fancy dates. She had just wanted to be with him.

Warren seemed different.

Not that this was a date. And besides, what seemed to be and what were … those could be two very different things.

Still, when Warren's lips curved into a smile at her compliment, she felt a zip of pleasure all the way to her toes. "Thanks for that, but my parents would probably disagree with you. I never quite seem to live up to their expectations for me."

How could he not? On the outside at least, Warren Kensington was handsome, philanthropic, successful—the whole package. "In what way?"

He rooted inside the box a bit, causing a few ornaments to clink together. "I'm thirty-seven and not married yet, for one." Finally, his hand emerged with a set of stocking ornaments that looked about as old as him. The red fabric was delicately stitched with white and gold threading that read Merry Christmas. Warren ran his finger over the words. "My younger sister fulfilled her duty to the family five years ago, but I've yet to produce an heir to the Kensington name."

"An heir." Kara rolled her eyes. "What is it with rich families and their obsession with carrying on the family name? Jeff was so insistent on having a boy for that very reason. It's not like you're royalty."

Too late, she realized her mistake. Kara covered her mouth with a hand. "Oh, I'm sorry." She shouldn't have criticized Warren's family or social sphere.

Warren stepped closer and Kara couldn't help it —she flinched. Because after a remark like that, Jeff would have backhanded her to next Sunday.

"Hey." The tender word reached out, feathering Kara's cheeks.

When she peeked at Warren, he was close. Still giving her space, but not quite as much as before. She bit her lip. "I shouldn't have said that."

His eyes crinkled at the corners. "Why not? I happen to agree with you."

Her chest loosened. "Really?"

A nod. "I only wish my parents did too. Then

maybe they'd lay off their search for my future wife and let me live my life in peace."

She shouldn't ask—it was absolutely none of her business—but Kara couldn't help herself. "So … you don't want to get married?"

He studied her, his gaze skimming her cheeks before meeting her own. "Actually, I'd love nothing more than to have a family to come home to at night. Kids to wrestle with, to read to at bedtime." Warren adjusted an ornament that wasn't crooked. "A wife to partner with. One who wants me for more than …" He paused.

"More than what?"

"Ah, never mind." Shrugging, he gave her a wry smile. "I just haven't found someone worth giving my everything to yet … no one who's willing to give hers in return, anyway."

CHAPTER 5

ad Kara ever known the meaning of the word "tired" before today?

She stepped into Once Upon a Time Bakery and allowed her exhausted muscles to thaw in the heated room filled with patrons. The light of the day had faded a few hours ago, and with the disappearance of the sun had come an unexpected chill. Snow was in the forecast this weekend, but thankfully not until after tomorrow, when her guests would begin arriving.

This was only her second time inside the small bakery, since she'd stopped by once yesterday morning to grab a box of cookies before heading out to Pendolphin House with Joy and Sarah for a day of decorating. Funnily enough, the bakery—with modern yellow-accented decor arranged behind the long counter, large metal whisks that had been made into light fixtures, and gray-and-white, diamond-patterned tile—wasn't exactly Kara's style, but something about the place instantly felt like a piece of home.

That very well could be due to the owner. Sarah's sister, Ginny, had lived in England for nearly a decade but was still American at heart.

"Kara! Welcome back." Ginny waved from behind the cash register, a wide grin on her face as she gestured Kara closer.

Kara should have expected that in a town as small as this, she couldn't simply stop in to grab a late-night coffee without being noticed. Too bad, because all she wanted to do at the moment was snag a hot bath at the B&B and hunker down in her pajamas next to the window in her bedroom—after all, it had been another brutal day of working through details at Pendolphin House.

The rest of the board had arrived a day earlier than the paying guests, and many of them had had questions for Kara. So, she'd spent a large part of her day sequestered in the Pendolphin boardroom outlining not only her plan for this weekend's fundraiser, but also upcoming fundraisers and donor relations efforts that would garner even more donations next year.

And the whole time, she'd tried to ignore the

stupid way her heart had skipped a beat every time she'd caught Warren's eye. His words two evenings ago still made the rounds in her head anytime she had two seconds alone: *I just haven't found someone worth giving my everything to yet ... no one who's willing to give hers in return, anyway.*

Oy. Exhausted was an understatement. But coffee could help with that, so instead of retreating, Kara worked up a smile. "Hey, Ginny. How are things here?"

"Booming, as you can see." Ginny bounced on her toes, her long brown ponytail springing with her movement. "It's as wonderful as chocolate and peanut butter blended together."

Kara couldn't help but laugh. She and Sarah may be sisters, but Ginny's youthful exuberance was quite different than Sarah's more stoic nature. "That is quite wonderful, I must say."

"Isn't it, though?" Ginny cocked her head and tugged on the long sleeves of her Beatles T-shirt. "I still can't believe my life sometimes. I've got my dream job, working next door to my best friend."

Ah yes, Rosebud Books was next to the bakery—in fact, a door between them allowed customers to flow more easily from one business to the other—and the owner was Sophia Rose, who was married to William. They had an almost-three-year-old named Emily and a four-month-old son, Edward. Kara had met them all yesterday when she'd snuck over and spent an hour perusing the bookstore's offerings.

Ginny continued. "And then, I got a second chance at love despite a rocky divorce. Now, Steven and I are in the process of adopting a little girl from London." She sighed, contentment written all over her face. "God has been really good to me."

Something in Kara's heart leaped at hearing Ginny's story—from the pit of devastation to this.

Could that ever be her?

But Ginny had credited God with her happiness. No offense to her, but Kara had to learn to stand on her own, and that meant depending on no one else—especially someone who hadn't answered her prayers in the past.

"Sorry, you didn't come here to hear how great my life is." The bakery owner chuckled. "What can I get for you tonight?"

"Just an americano, please."

Ginny took Kara's payment, then saluted. "Feel free to take a seat. My sister's tucked away in the corner if you need someone to sit with. I'll bring your coffee over when it's ready." Before Kara had a chance to thank her, the brunette turned on her heel and headed for the gleaming espresso machine.

Sarah was here? Kara turned and studied the crowded bakery. Sure enough, there sat her boss behind her laptop, a half-eaten blueberry scone and a teal mug on the table beside her. Kara made her way over. "Still burning the midnight oil?"

Sarah peeked up, smiled. "Always." She shut her laptop, moved it aside, and gestured to the seat across the booth. "Join me?"

"I don't want to interrupt. Just stopped in for a coffee." Kara rubbed the back of her neck where she'd had a crick since waking up this morning.

"You aren't interrupting, but I completely understand if you'd rather head straight back to your room." Sarah tilted her head. "I'd love to hear how your day went if you can spare a few minutes, though."

"Of course." Kara slid into the booth, the coolness of which seeped through her skinny jeans. "Today was great. As you saw yesterday, Meg has everything well in hand. I spent most of my time with the board." She updated Sarah on the details of the day. By the time she was finished, Ginny had dropped off her americano in a ceramic mug.

Oops. She'd forgotten to get it to go. Oh well. Sarah didn't look overly eager to get back to her work. "What about you? How was your day?" She lifted the mug to her lips and sipped. The sweet and bitter combination of the beans and milk toasted her insides.

Sarah gnawed at her bottom lip. "I'm helping Melissa with a tricky case that reminds me a lot of yours." She cocked her head. "Is that okay to tell you? I don't want to make things harder for you. I imagine it's already an emotional time of year."

The concern in her boss's eyes nearly undid Kara, and she gripped the mug with both hands, staring into the dark brew. Yes, December did not bring with it the most pleasant of memories.

There was the fear, of course—once she'd made the decision to leave Jeff, she'd waited until he was out of town and called her sister to come to help her pack and get out of the house.

But then had come the uncertainty, the doubt over whether she'd even done the right thing.

The worry over whether she'd lose Rose.

That's when the nightmares had started.

Sure, over the last few years, they'd tapered off some, but she still woke with fairly regular frequency drenched in sweat, her heart running a marathon, wondering if she'd screamed out loud the same way she'd been screaming in her dream.

Kara cleared her throat. "I'm fine. Sorry you're dealing with such a hard case."

"I just wish I could do more, you know?"

"More? Sarah, you've dedicated your whole life to helping women like me get out of bad situations." She'd *saved* Kara. "What more could you possibly do?"

Sharp, loud laughter rose from the table next to

them—two older women having a grand old time, from the sound of it.

Sarah waited until they quieted to say anything. "It just never feels like enough."

Behind Kara, the bell over the door jangled. At the noise, Sarah glanced up and her frown quickly turned into a grin. She waved. "Michael! Warren!"

Warren was here? Kara couldn't help but sink a little lower into her seat as she white-knuckled her mug.

Sarah noticed the movement and narrowed her gaze. "What's wrong?"

"Nothing." Kara inwardly groaned at the crack in her voice. *Please don't ask again.*

But Sarah was a lawyer—she didn't let stuff go. The woman placed her elbows on the table and leaned forward, lowering her voice. "Is something going on between you and Warren?"

"What? No!" Kara peeked around the corner of the booth. Michael, whose unruly brown curls were stuck underneath a beanie, and Warren were chatting with Ginny at the counter. Kara had a minute, maybe two, before they made their way over here. What excuse could she give for leaving when they did?

Being tired was always a good reason—and true. The problem was, if she said she needed to go, Warren might try to be chivalrous and escort her home. Then there would be an awkward few moments of being alone with him—moments she'd need to fill with conversation.

And for some reason, conversation with Warren tended to get serious quickly. Could she really afford another evening of delving into matters of the heart with him?

Sarah studied her, one eyebrow raised. "I dated Warren once upon a time, you know."

Kara's mouth fell open. That was definitely not what she'd expected to hear. "What? When? Why?"

"Colonel Mustard in the library with the wrench." Sarah's lips twisted into a wry grin. "Sorry, it just suddenly felt like we were playing Clue."

Kara allowed herself a laugh. "Ha ha."

"Anyway, Warren and I went out on a few dates three years ago. He even followed me out here when I came for a visit to make amends with Ginny. A grand gesture of sorts."

Oh, right. The month-long trip Sarah had taken just after Kara had left Jeff. She nodded. "What happened?"

"Michael did." Now Sarah looked past Kara, presumably at her husband, who must still be ordering something and talking with his sister-in-law. "Once we met, my heart belonged to him, no matter how good of a guy Warren was."

She paused, returning her focus to Kara. "And he *is* a good guy, Kara. I'd trust him with my life. In fact …" Sarah shook her head. "Suffice it to say that New

Dawn wouldn't have survived without him. He's one of the good ones. So, if you were ever interested—"

"I'm not." Kara swigged her coffee, the liquid—and the lie—burning a trail down her throat.

"Okay, okay. I get it. You've been hurt. Majorly. No one would blame you for not trusting easily again." Her boss reached out, patted Kara's hand. "But I'm just saying. If—hopefully when—you decide you are ready to get back out there, you can't do better than Warren Kensington."

Before Kara could respond, the man himself—and Michael, a gregarious smile on his face—sauntered up, mugs in hand. They both greeted the women warmly and asked if they could join them.

Sarah glanced at Kara. "Did you still need to get home?"

Bless her. She was giving Kara an easy out.

But something about their conversation niggled, making Kara not quite as anxious to retreat to her lonely room. She may have trouble trusting men, but she trusted Sarah more than anyone in her life, save her sister. And if Sarah said Warren was a good guy ...

Besides, staying didn't mean Kara was opening her heart to a relationship. Staying merely meant she was open to good conversations with friends.

Old friends ... and new ones too.

She chewed the inside of her cheek before

shaking her head. "I can stay for a bit." Then she slid over, finally peeking up at Warren. "Sit if you'd like."

And his responding smile was like coming out of the cold and into a cozy, heated room with a fire crackling in the corner.

Kara only prayed that she wouldn't get burned.

CHAPTER 6

The first guest could arrive at any moment.

Kara paced the entryway of Pendolphin House, which served as a foyer of sorts. A large registration desk sat in front of a paneled wall, nestled between two sweeping staircases that led to the second and third stories of the manor. Thick brocade rugs in deep maroons and golds adorned the wood floors and lent a certain luxury to the place. Everywhere Kara looked, there seemed to be some nook or cranny that held a treasure from the past—portraits of men and women long gone, vases with flowers frozen in time, old wing-backed chairs with faded fabric.

The guest rooms were equally as elegant, with beds that featured rosewood canopy beds and matching bedside tables, dressing tables with curved mirrors, and chests of drawers. Even Kara's room—a tiny space tucked away in the servants' quarters—was adorable with its pale green floral-patterned wallpaper and lacy coverlet. Of course, she'd been sad to leave Rebecca's behind, but it made much more sense for her to stay here in case one of the guests needed something that she could help with. Besides, she'd get to return to Rebecca's after the fundraiser ended, now that she'd decided to stay through Christmas. Last night, Sarah and company had convinced her.

And her decision had absolutely nothing to do with the fact Warren was also staying on through Christmas.

Nothing.

"Ma'am, I really do have this handled if you want to relax." Gwen, a twenty-something who worked for Meg at Pendolphin House, arched a thinly plucked eyebrow Kara's direction—specifically, at the way her heels were probably wearing a path in the old floorboards.

Kara withheld a sigh and smiled instead. "Of course you do." After all, Meg seemed confident in Gwen's abilities to get everyone checked in just fine, and the woman hadn't let Kara down yet. "I'm just here to help if you need me."

She hoped her presence would lend even more credence to New Dawn's cause. Donors liked to feel welcomed, special. And this wasn't just some five-course fundraising dinner they'd committed themselves to. No, this was an entire weekend. It was imperative that these guests be wooed and kept— that they loved the experience so much they told all of their friends about it and encouraged them to become donors too.

A lot more was riding on this than Gwen knew, so Kara would stay right here, thank you very much.

The rumble of a car engine emanated from outside. Someone was here. Kara's insides tightened as she stopped her pacing, hurried to the staircase, and tried to stand casually next to it. There went the lift in Gwen's eyebrow again as she no doubt had some thought about crazy Americans. Before Kara could think of something to say to lighten the mood between them, the large dark front door swung open.

Showtime.

In walked Warren, looking somewhat windswept as he rolled a small suitcase behind him and slid off his overcoat. He caught sight of her and flashed her a dimpled grin. "Afternoon."

"Hi." Kara's stupid voice chose that moment to squeak as if she were in junior high.

But honestly. A man really had no right looking that handsome.

What? No, no, no. Kara's cheeks burned at the thought—but maybe it was natural, this attraction. After all, he was a good guy. Sarah's ringing endorsement and everything Kara had witnessed said as much.

And that goodness made him all the more attractive.

Even now, as he checked into his room, he treated Gwen with the utmost respect—friendly but not flirtatious.

And last night, they'd spent a few hours chatting with Sarah and Michael about everything from work and New Dawn to their favorite vacation spots to kids. Warren had entertained them with stories of his nephew and niece and his escapades in changing a diaper for the first time when babysitting last year.

But she didn't have time to think any more warm —and slightly uncomfortable—thoughts about Warren, because another couple swooped in while Gwen was helping him. Kara moved forward to assist the woman with her bag. Didn't they have a bellhop here? She thought she'd seen one, but he didn't seem to be at his station. "Let me get that."

"Oh, thank you, dear." The woman appeared to be in her sixties or seventies, her refined white hair perfectly styled and coiffed. From her head to her Louboutin-ed toes, she oozed money. "The traffic from London was simply atrocious, and on a Thursday, no less. But we are here now and oh so happy to have a weekend away."

The man standing beside her didn't reply to his wife's chatter—just frowned and wiggled his gray mustache. Then, "How long does it take to get checked in around here?" His impatient British accent filled the space despite the high ceiling.

Out of the corner of her eye, Kara saw Gwen stiffen. Thankfully, though, Meg had trained her employee well because she didn't lash out or say anything, really. She simply kept helping Warren, detailing the week's events and where to find the manor's restaurant.

Hopefully Kara could smooth any ruffled feathers before the grumbling got worse. She surged forward, hand outstretched. "I'm Kara Gentry, the special events coordinator for New Dawn."

The man stared at her hand for a moment before shaking it. "What's New Dawn?"

His wife rolled her eyes. "It's the charity we're here to support, you oaf."

"I thought you dragged me out here to celebrate our anniversary."

"I'm not sure it's worth celebrating after all." The woman turned her nose in the air.

Well, this was devolving quickly. Kara cleared her throat. "I'm sorry, I didn't catch your names."

"Robert and Bobbi Clyde, dear." The woman shot her husband a "be nice" glare before taking Kara's hand between her own. Her skin was cold, her fingers adorned with several rings, including a monstrosity that had to be at least three carats.

Despite the man's poor behavior, these were

exactly the sort of people Kara needed here. They had deep pockets and were willing to give some of their money to charity. But his mannerisms—the superiority, the rudeness—reminded Kara of why she was glad to no longer be part of the upper echelons of society, at least in her personal life.

And Warren … well, this was his world.

Which was one big reason to stop the line of thinking that might lead her to consider him as anything other than the president of her workplace's board of directors. And, fine, maybe as a friend.

She could do friendship, right?

Kara snuck a glance at him as he grabbed his room key from Gwen and turned her way, the gleam of his glasses catching the light and his chiseled jaw looking as rock-solid as ever.

Friends. Right.

Maybe?

He approached. "Did I hear you say you're the Clydes?"

The man seemed to puff out his chest a bit. "Depends. Who's asking?"

"Warren Kensington, sir."

Robert harrumphed. "I believe your father and I went to school together." But there seemed to be a crack in his defenses. Unbelievable, the connections that a Bostonian had across the pond—all because they belonged to the same social class.

"They did. He has told me many a story of your antics together. And how smart you are."

"Yes, well." Robert finally took Warren's hand and pumped it up and down.

Warren turned to Bobbi, reaching for her hand and kissing it. "It's a pleasure to finally meet you, ma'am."

She giggled. "Oh, the pleasure is all ours."

"Indeed." Stroking his mustache, Robert nodded. "We should chat more. I'd love to hear what your father has been up to these days."

Kara had been all but forgotten—probably as it should be. She took a few steps back. Another couple had walked in the front door and were headed for the registration desk, anyway.

Warren continued. "Let's get you both checked in and situated, and then I'd love to talk." He glanced at Kara. "Kara, won't you join us? I'm sure the Clydes would love to hear all about New Dawn and how their contributions have helped countless women in horrific circumstances."

The sincerity in his tone, the light in his eyes, the smile on his lips ... he was helping her do what she couldn't on her own. And while she hated that she needed an "in" in the first place, she also couldn't help smiling in return, expressing her gratitude with a mouthed "thank you" when the Clydes weren't looking.

And then, Warren winked at her—and her knees

felt like those of a baby giraffe, just born, not knowing how it had gotten there.

Friends, Kara. Just friends.

Oh, goodness. She was in trouble.

The Clydes smiled and agreed to Warren's proposition, so he helped them get checked in while Kara greeted the fresh influx of guests. Gwen was swamped but handling it like a pro, so Kara wandered to the expansive kitchen and prepped some Earl Grey tea, which she placed on an adorable platter along with some "biscuits"—also known as cookies in the United States.

Then she made her way to the lobby-slash-library, where Warren sat with the Clydes. Kara set the tea tray onto the coffee table and placed a hand against her chest as she took in the sights around her. How had she missed the grandeur of this room on her tour? She must have been so caught up in the details of the event that she hadn't noticed the painted teal walls, the sparkling chandelier over-head, the cozy-looking settees and couches and chairs, the adorably Victorian fireplace—and the rows and rows of dusty old books.

The *Beauty and the Beast*-loving girl in her—who had envied Belle her library—wanted to squeal.

Of course, Kara was much too distinguished for that, so she tamped down her inner enthusiasm and turned to the guests with a smile as she lowered herself into a chair beside Warren. "I brought some tea to warm you up. It's getting chilly outside."

"Thank you, dear. How thoughtful." Bobbi's smile was genuine enough, despite her grumpy husband. Although, actually, the lines of the man's face had seemed to ease here among the books. Perhaps he was merely uncomfortable in new places, in crowds, in awkward social situations.

She could at least give him the benefit of the doubt. Not everyone was like Jeff, after all—Warren least of all. He proved that much when he leaned forward and helped pour the tea. Their hands brushed and Kara sucked in a sharp breath at the contact, but Warren didn't seem to notice. He just kept chatting up the Clydes, keeping their conversation light, airy, comfortable.

He seemed to have that happy knack with everyone, didn't he? But it wasn't smarmy or slick, like Jeff, who was always looking to gain an advantage in the conversation. Warren seemed genuinely interested in others and their lives.

It was a welcome—albeit confusing—quality to observe in someone.

"Kara, I've told the Clydes a little about New Dawn, but I think you could probably do it more justice."

The warm look in her new friend's eyes once more stole her breath and made her mouth go dry, but she pushed past the discomfort. For the next half hour, she detailed the work they did at New Dawn—even hinting at her own story. Mr. Clyde remained quite silent, while his wife murmured and hmmed at several points.

When Kara sat back in her chair and took a sip of her tepid tea, Mr. Clyde finally spoke. "Well, young lady, I must confess that you've moved the heart of this old codger. I'd like nothing more than to give an extra donation to your worthy cause."

And when he named the amount, Kara nearly fell out of her chair. "Sir, you have no idea how many women you will be helping." Tears stung the backs of her eyes. "Thank you."

"Now, now." Robert stood. "Bobbi, my old bones need a rest in our room. Are you coming?"

His wife stood and patted his arm. "You old coot. Of course I am." Then they shuffled out of the room.

Kara shook her head as she watched them go. "That was … incredible." Biting her lip, she glanced at Warren. "Thank you."

"Hey." He held up his hands. "That was all you. You convinced them to donate."

"You got my foot in the door."

"We make a good team, then." He cocked his head, pausing, as if he wanted to say more.

Kara's heart picked up. Did she want to hear it? She glanced away, toward the fireplace, which was void of fire. Cold.

Thankfully, before she was forced to make a

decision for better or worse, Gwen swept into the room. "Ms. Gentry, we have a problem, and I can't get ahold of Meg." The woman's voice was tight, unsure for the first time since Kara had met her.

"Call me Kara. And breathe, Gwen." Kara jumped up and met her halfway, snagging her hand and squeezing. "What's going on?"

"The Chestertons showed up wanting an extra room for their friends—the Galbraiths, I believe. They were sure we could accommodate them despite not having a reservation." Gwen leaned in. "But when I tried explaining that all the guest rooms are taken, you'd have thought I'd murdered their best friend. The looks I got ..."

Kara's stomach twisted. The Chestertons were huge donors—one of their first supporting families for the London office. They couldn't afford to upset them. She pushed her fingers against her temples and paced. "Think, think." There had to be a solution.

Was it just her, or had the heater kicked on? Her silk blouse clung to her back, which was beginning to sweat.

"Might I make a suggestion?"

She halted and looked at Warren, who was now standing. "You've already rescued me once today." Which she hated in a way—what must he think of her ability to do this job?

But he just ribbed her slightly with his elbow and

smiled. Then he faced Gwen. "Are there any other rooms in the servants' quarters?"

"Yes …" Gwen's hesitation was clear.

And for good reason. Kara shook her head. "We cannot put the Chestertons' friends in an attic bedroom. For one thing, a double bed is much too small for a couple. And there's a fireplace, but it's still a bit on the chilly side up there."

"That's true. And the furnishings are more plain since we don't regularly rent those rooms out," Gwen added. "It's just the staff who uses them."

Warren chuckled. "I wasn't proposing we stick the Galbraiths up there. If it's the Galbraiths I know, that would never work. Let's just say they're used to the finer things." His eyebrows waggled as he touched the side of his nose.

"Then what *are* you saying?" Kara asked.

"Give them my room and I'll stay in the attic. Simple as that."

"Warren …" She frowned. "We couldn't ask you to do that."

He shrugged. "You're not asking. I'm volunteering. I don't need much. Just somewhere to lay my head and plug in my electronics."

One thing was certain—Jeff would *never* offer to give up his room for the good of the charity or someone else.

No, make that two things. Kara was also certain that she shouldn't be comparing Jeff and Warren.

That would mean she was looking at Warren as more than a friend.

As a … possibility. For more.

And well, that might just spell disaster. She'd trusted a rich man before, and her heart had been broken. Even if Warren and Jeff were different—she could now admit that Warren was not someone who was likely to abuse her—how did she know that he wouldn't betray her trust in some other way?

No, remaining single was just … better. Easier.

But as she followed Gwen out of the room to sort out the mess up front, Kara couldn't help but wonder if her definition of "easy" would someday bring her heartache of a different kind.

One minute, Kara was back there—in *his* house.

Cowering in the corner.

Begging him to stop.

Pleading with him to return to the man she'd fallen in love with.

The next, she was jolting upright in bed, her hair clinging to the back of her neck, a scream reverberating through the still night.

Kara's heart clattered around in her chest. Would these nightmares ever go away? It was something she and her therapist were slowly working on, but there were no easy answers.

A knock on her door nearly had her crying out again. "Kara?" It was just one word, but she couldn't miss the care in Warren's voice. Now that his room was next to hers, she must have woken him with her screaming. Thankfully, they were the only two staying on this floor of the house. She prayed that meant no one else had been disturbed.

Kara climbed from her bed, wincing when her bare feet touched the cold floor. She pulled her sweatshirt on over her pajamas—a PTA T-shirt and pale pink lounge pants—before pattering to the door.

Warren stood there in the same white shirt and sweatpants she'd seen him in the other morning at Rebecca's. The moonlight streaming through one of the upper-floor hallway windows revealed that he was squinting at her. "Hey." Despite his lack of eyewear, he peeked into her room, scanning it as if looking for intruders. "You okay?" His voice was on the breathless side.

"I'm fine." Kara snagged a strand of hair and tugged on it, smoothing it with her thumb and fore-finger. No doubt she looked less than gorgeous with her tangled mane, smudged mascara she'd forgotten to remove last night, and baggy clothing. Jeff had joked more than once that he didn't recognize her in the morning before she put on her face. "Sorry to wake you up. Just a nightmare."

Warren's jaw flexed at her answer. Sticking his hands into the pockets of his sweatpants, he leaned against the door frame. "Do you get those often?"

To admit her weakness or not? That was the question. But there had always been something mystical about nighttime—for some reason, it was easier to talk about things. Easier to be vulnerable.

Easier to forget that, in the light of day, a person had to live with the consequences of opening up.

Still, despite her better judgment, Kara found herself wanting to answer him honestly. "More than I'd like."

He waited for a few beats before saying more. "I don't know about you, but I'm fully awake now. How about some hot chocolate or tea to calm our nerves?"

Clearly Warren was just being kind, but he was right—there was no going back to sleep right now. And a hot drink did sound tempting …

So did spending time with Warren.

But what about the resolution she'd made earlier this evening to stay single?

He's not asking you to marry him, silly. Just to get something to drink.

Right. She was thirty-eight years old. A mom. Not some young ingenue obsessed with the idea of love. She could have a drink—and a non-alcoholic one, at that—with a man without losing her self-control. "Hot chocolate sounds nice. Thanks."

"Let me just go get my glasses. Be right back."

"I'll meet you in the kitchen."

"No, no. You've worked hard all day. Let me get the drinks, then I'll bring them to the library. Deal?"

Kara bit her bottom lip to hide her smile. "All right." Even though she definitely didn't need it, it felt nice to have someone take care of her. As he strode down the hall toward his room, Kara grabbed her room key and headed for the stairs.

The rest of the guests were tucked away in their rooms, likely sleeping hard after a day of travel, a delicious buffet dinner served in the dining room, and an evening of cocktails and cards in the drawing room. As Kara had made the rounds, it'd seemed like many people already knew each other—again, not surprising given their status and the fact most of them lived in London. Some, however, hailed from Scotland, Ireland, and Wales, and one couple had come all the way from Paris. The conversation had been lively and friendly, and many of those in attendance took the time to talk with Kara about their passion for New Dawn's mission—a conversation led primarily by Bobbi Clyde.

Now, the library was quiet and dark as Kara entered. Instead of illuminating the chandelier, she allowed the moon and the hall light to be enough as she made her way to the fireplace she'd admired earlier. Feeling along the wall, she found the switch and flipped it to ignite the gas fire. Pendolphin House may appear to be a complete step back in time, but thankfully it had been upgraded in a few ways.

Kara settled into one of the chairs facing the fire and breathed in the scent of old books all around her, allowing the hidden words in the stories to penetrate her spirit, to bolster her.

There were times that she felt she'd moved past what Jeff had done to her. Other times—like right now—she wondered if she'd always be a little bit broken.

And no man could ever want someone like that. Especially a man like Warren Kensington, a guy with the world at his fingertips. Someone who could have any woman he desired.

Not that it mattered. They were friends. And the comfort and hot chocolate? He was just being sweet to her. Didn't mean he was sweet *on* her.

"Here we go." The man in question emerged from behind Kara, two mugs in hand. Gently, he set one on the side table between their chairs, then lowered himself into the other wingback without spilling a drop.

"Thanks." Taking the offered mug, she sipped—and nearly groaned with delight. "This is wonderful."

"You like it?"

"Who wouldn't?" The liquid chocolate was like a

gorgeous warm river of silk flowing down her throat. "Did you make this or was the baker in the kitchen?" She'd heard that the woman who made the pastries and bread for the house kept early hours, so perhaps that explained the total divinity in her mug.

Warren cleared his throat. "I did. It was my grandmother's recipe, and luckily the kitchen had everything I needed."

"You keep surprising me." Her words came out low and throaty, which was not her intention. But they were true.

Warren's eyebrows arched over his glasses. "Really? How so?" A chunk of his hair—normally so styled and in place—stuck out behind his ear.

Kara's hand itched to tamp it down, but she held fast to the handle of her mug instead. "I don't know. Most guys who can afford a cook are happy to let the staff handle all food preparation. Why do for yourself what you can pay someone else to do? That's always been Jeff's motto, anyway." She shrugged and sipped her drink again.

"No offense, Kara, but I hope you know that I'm nothing like your good-for-nothing ex-husband."

Mid-sip, she choked a bit. Her cheeks warm, she glanced up at Warren, who was staring at her so intently, she had to look away. The flames of the fire flicked and undulated in front of her, an unsteady rhythm to their dance. "That's not what I meant."

"It kind of sounds like you did." His gentle tone

didn't keep her from feeling the admonishment in his words. No, not admonishment.

Hurt.

But still she couldn't face him. "I just …" Her lip trembled. "I've spent a lot of time in your world, but I never really belonged."

"Why do you say that?"

"Jeff never knew this about me, but I grew up poor. Like, really poor." And why was she telling Warren this? But once she'd started, the story rolled from her lips. "When I was twelve, my mom ended up dating and marrying a man she worked for. He was on the wealthy side—not as rich as Jeff, but well off."

Tom had been a smooth talker. So smooth that Kara had believed him when he'd denied cheating on her mother. Denied calling her terrible names. Denied lying to all of them.

Kara took another drink, remembering how unstable her life had been growing up. How she'd craved safety. Security.

How she'd sought it in all the wrong places.

First, in her stepdad, who had showered her with fatherly affection she'd never had before.

Then, in a man like Jeff Gentry.

Both men had ended up liars. Frauds. Betrayers of the worst kind.

"But Tom abandoned us after our mom died." For whatever reason, after her mother's death, he'd written both Kara and Cindy out of his will, leaving every penny of his money to a son from his first marriage. Thankfully, Cindy had already married Travis, and Kara had started working after college, so they didn't need his money. But the fact he hadn't even thought to provide for them still stung.

Kara cleared her throat. "So it was up to me to forge a new path on my own. No one had to know my true past. I'd risen from 'trailer trash' to the stepdaughter of a wealthy man, and I got really good at pretending I belonged. When I met Jeff at a charity event my firm had sent me to, he saw my poise, knew my former association with my stepdad, and just assumed that's who I was. And I didn't contradict him." She huffed out a breath. "I openly lived a lie because I was too afraid to tell people the truth of where I'd come from."

"Not sure I'd call that a lie, per se," Warren said. "People put so much emphasis on class, but what really matters is who you are on the inside."

She blinked, the fire almost blinding in its stark brightness against the dark wisps of night. "You're right, of course. It wasn't necessarily the fact that I had *been* poor, more that I was ashamed of it. I thought it made me less worthy of love, like I had to work ten times harder to be seen, to succeed, to find a man who thought I was special."

There she went again, being a Chatty Cathy. Goodness. What was with her tonight?

Other than her therapist and Cindy, Kara had never said any of this to … anyone. So why Warren? Why now? She swallowed, hard, and gathered the courage to look at him again. "I was so desperate to be loved that I let myself fall for a monster. Not that I knew who he was at first. But six months into our marriage, it was clear that I wasn't the only one who had been hiding a part of myself away."

"I'm sorry, Kara." His lips twisted into a deep frown. "I really can't even imagine what that must have been like. And I'm sorry he hurt you. But look at you. You are here, and you're surviving."

"But I'm not thriving." The truth of it nearly strangled her. "And I want that more than anything."

"You'll get there."

"How can you be so sure?" She scooted forward in her chair, whispering the words, a plea for him to reveal a bit of truth she'd somehow missed.

"Because you're brave. Anyone who has endured what you have and is still standing, still fighting … that's a woman I'm proud to know." He paused. "A woman I'm proud to … be friends with."

Friends. Right.

Kara swiped at invisible tears. She took another swig of the chocolate, now significantly cooled but no less tasty. Time to change the subject. "What about you? How did you get involved with New Dawn?"

Warren rubbed the back of his neck. "I've always

had a soft spot for charities that helped battered women and children. My grandfather was a hard man who abused my grandmother."

"Oh, I'm sorry."

He nodded, his lips in a straight line. "She lived with it for a long time and didn't tell her story until he'd died. But she shouldn't have had to live with it at all." When he looked at her, there was something apologetic in his gaze. "None of you should."

She couldn't speak. Could only swallow.

And suddenly she realized they were both leaning across the arms of their chairs. If she came two more inches, if he did, then they'd be in each other's space.

Close enough to kiss.

If she wanted to.

The air between them shifted. Something pulsed and moved and breathed—something Kara hadn't felt in oh so long.

Hope.

Anticipation.

The wonder of what could be.

But those were dangerous for a woman like her— because hope led places she wasn't sure she could ever go again.

Kara cleared her throat and sat back against the opposite arm of her chair, as far away from Warren as she could get without leaving her seat. "That explains your passion for New Dawn's work, but not how you got involved with them specifically." A pause. "Sarah said something about New Dawn not surviving without you. What did she mean?"

"Oh." He shrugged and placed his mug on the side table. "Sarah's exaggerating. With a determined woman like her in charge, it would have survived with or without me."

"Okay, but still. What made you get involved— and not just as a donor, but the president of the board?"

Shifting in his seat, Warren scraped a hand through his unruly hair. Was he nervous? But why? "You."

Oh. "Me?"

"Or rather, your case. Sarah's father said if she didn't drop it, he would cut off his sizable donation. Apparently Jeff was a good friend of his."

Kara gasped. "What?"

Warren nodded. "Of course, Sarah refused, but she was worried about New Dawn surviving without his purse strings."

"I never meant to cause so much trouble." She'd just been desperate, with nowhere else to turn.

"Kara." He waited until their eyes met again. "You've never been trouble, okay? If anything, you spurred me into action. I'd seen you from afar, admired all you did for the charity events community, and when I heard that your husband was hurting you ..." Warren gripped the side of his chair.

"I felt so helpless, Kara. Here was a guy I knew hurting someone—his wife, no less—and there were other men in my circle keeping quiet about it. Rallying around him like a good old boy, determined to 'protect their own.' Frankly, it still makes me sick just thinking about it."

Oh, Warren. "You didn't have to—"

"I did." Even in the dim light, she saw the flash in his eyes. Of determination—and something else. "I may have been born into a wealthy family, but that does not get to dictate the kind of man I am. That day, when I saw Sarah's passion for you, for survivors like you, I knew that I could do something too—even if it was just giving my money. I have plenty of it. Why not use it for something that changes people's lives in a tangible way?"

His words … beautiful.

But Kara had to turn away. Had to get out of here. Now.

Because hope was doing a pesky tap dance on her heart—and Kara had the strongest urge to throw open the doors. She was becoming weaker and weaker to Warren Kensington's charms.

And in this moment, with the moonlight making memories hazy, she couldn't remember exactly why that was a bad thing.

CHAPTER 7

"Excuse me, dear."

Kara turned from her place behind the registration desk to find a regal-looking elderly British woman—maybe in her eighties—next to a younger woman. Mrs. Doyle and her granddaughter, if memory served.

Gwen had run off for a few minutes to the restroom, leaving Kara to direct guests to their Friday evening activities. "Yes? How may I help you?"

The younger woman stepped forward. "We saw in the brochure you provided that tonight there's a Winter Walk in the village." She pushed a strand of auburn hair behind her ear, exposing a diamond earring, a funny contrast with her jeans and leather jacket. "Can you tell us more about that?"

"Of course." Kara had been fielding questions

about the walk all day long, so the details came easily to her mind. "The Winter Walk is rather new. Several business owners in town decided it would be a fun way to gather everyone together the weekend before Christmas. They've strung lights all over town and are keeping the shops open later than usual."

"Oh, fabulous. We haven't quite finished our Christmas shopping, have we, Jayne?" Mrs. Doyle winked at her granddaughter, who bit her lip shyly and shook her head.

Kara smiled. What a lovely pair of women. "You'll also want to stop by the tree lighting ceremony at seven. It will take place in the community park just off Fifth and High Street, and the local bakery is providing free treats and hot cider for everyone."

"Sounds magical." Sighing, the younger woman patted her grandma's hand. "I think we should go, don't you, Gran?"

"I do, if I can stay awake that late." Together, they laughed and shuffled off after thanking Kara.

Ensuring that no one else needed her, Kara turned back to her phone. After a quick chat with Rose—who was supposed to leave for her cruise in two days—she'd been texting with Cindy. Her sister's latest text had left Kara wondering how to best answer it.

Cindy: So, how much of Warren Kensington are you seeing?

Too much.

Was that an answer? Yes, but it would spark all kinds of extra questions that Kara wasn't ready to answer. Biting her lip, she set the phone back down.

The bell on the counter rang and Kara's hand flew to her chest as she swiveled.

Warren stood there, a sheepish grin on his lips. "Didn't mean to startle you."

Kara lowered her hand and straightened her shoulders, praying she looked nonchalant—and not guilty for the previous line of her thoughts. "You didn't."

After their talk last night—this morning?—she'd mostly avoided him today. But Kara couldn't forget the way he'd walked her to her room, leaned against the door frame once more, and whispered good night without a single attempt to kiss her.

She also couldn't forget the sinking in her stomach at the realization that she kind of wished he had tried.

Ugh. Why couldn't she get a grip on her stupid emotions?

Before Warren could answer, several groups of people worked their way toward the front door, chattering loudly. She gave a quick glimpse at the clock. Six already? The day had flown by, but that's what happened when running an event. Thankfully, all the details seemed to be taken care of for tomorrow night's ball—all that she could handle for now, anyway. Tomorrow was another story. Once all the vendors arrived, she and Meg would be busy bees.

Warren placed his elbows on the counter and leaned forward, glimpsing the brochure Kara had distributed to the guests. "So, this Winter Walk … is it new?"

She nodded. "I heard Ginny wanted to mimic something they do in Nantucket, although on a much smaller scale. I guess she grew up going there a bunch as a kid."

"Oh, yeah. That's actually where our families met. We vacationed there every summer."

Of course they had. Kara couldn't even imagine that kind of childhood. Until Mom had married Tom, Kara's summers had consisted of days watching TV at home or reading in the far corners of the public library alone while her mother and Cindy worked.

But that wasn't Warren's fault. Besides, those summer days had grown Kara's love of books, which had served as an escape during her marriage to Jeff.

Kara shook off the memories and returned her focus to the conversation at hand. "Anyway, Ginny and Sophia started the Winter Walk two years ago hoping it would bring in extra tourists from the surrounding villages and beyond. The restaurants and shops are offering discounts all weekend long and staying open later than usual. Since Joy is such good friends with Sophia, she suggested that we coordinate our fundraiser with the timing of the walk so our guests would have something extra special to do in town."

"That was very smart of you." Warren quirked an eyebrow. "I'm surprised you haven't left yet. The tree lighting begins soon."

"Oh, I'm not going." Or, she hadn't planned to. She'd been positive that she would be up until the wee hours of the morning prepping for the ball. But Meg's supreme efficiency had caught her off guard.

"Really?" Frowning, Warren swept his gaze around the entryway. "Seems to me there's not much left for you to do here."

Was it her imagination, or did it seem like he wanted her to go?

But she shouldn't. Right? Thankfully, she still had one excuse that would keep her from having to make a real decision. "Oh, well, Gwen needs me to help work the desk, so ..."

Of course, the woman chose that moment to round the corner, a huge smile on her face when she saw Warren. "How's my favorite guest doing tonight?"

"I'm fine, Gwen. And you?"

"I'd be better if I could get out of here and join you all at the tree lighting." She gave a sigh. "It sounds so romantic. Speaking of, why haven't the two of you left yet? You're going together, right?"

"What?" Kara choked on the word. Why was everyone—Cindy, Sarah, and now Gwen—trying to push her toward Warren? They were from different worlds, and he could never understand hers.

But a quick peek at him, and all her hot air deflated. It made sense. Warren was a good man. The fact he hadn't tried to kiss her last night—or find other ways to take advantage of her vulnerability—spoke to that. Or perhaps he genuinely wasn't interested in her like that.

Even though there were moments …

But whatever he felt, she couldn't deny it any longer.

Part of *her* was interested—the part that wasn't terrified he'd end up betraying her too.

And that part was starting to shout louder than the fear.

But it had been so long since she'd dated. Since she'd even considered dating. Although, going to a tree lighting ceremony—where the entire town, and her friends would be—wasn't really considered a date anyway, right? So maybe …

Kara squinted at Warren, who watched her closely. "When are you leaving?"

A huge grin found its way across his lips. "Want a ride?"

"I'd need to change first." Her dress pants and heels would hardly make for a comfortable time walking around town.

"I'll wait here."

"All right." Kara nodded at Gwen, who snuck a wink at her, then walked to the staircase. When she was out of everyone's sight, she hauled booty up the stairs to her room and tore open her suitcase. She didn't have much time to decide, so she went with her instincts—a pair of skinny jeans, knee-high leather boots, and a red sweater with a matching scarf.

As quickly as possible, she reapplied some mascara and lip gloss, then gave her sadly flat hair an upside-down shake and threw on her coat over it all.

There. Done. This wasn't a big deal. Just a tree lighting ceremony. In public. It was completely safe.

Not. A. Big. Deal.

But she couldn't fool herself—her insides were shaking.

Employing a few breathing techniques that her therapist had taught her, Kara looked in the mirror and spoke truths to herself—ones she mostly believed.

Some of the time.

Maybe.

Regardless. "Kara Gentry, you are smart. You are beautiful. You are worthy." Her voice wobbled over each word, but she kept going. "No man can give you the validation you seek. And you don't need it anyway. Your worth comes from elsewhere."

Satisfied, she punched out a text to Cindy—*Miss*

you! Let's chat soon.—and headed back downstairs where Warren sat on his phone in the corner of the entryway.

When he glanced up, his entire face—which had been scrunched in concentration—relaxed. He stuffed his phone into his pocket and stood. "You look great, Kara."

"Thanks. You too." She tried to keep from biting her lip, but wasn't successful. "Ready to go?"

"Let's do it."

They both waved to Gwen and headed out to the parking lot, where Warren walked them to a black SUV. It wasn't anything fancy, just sturdy and well built.

Kind of like Warren.

Oh, goodness. She had it bad.

Like the true gentleman he was, Warren opened Kara's door for her, then rounded the vehicle and climbed in on the other side. He cranked the heat. "It's supposed to snow tonight or tomorrow."

"I know." She held her hands up to the vents, but pulled them back when cool air blew out for the first few seconds. "I've been stalking the weather reports, afraid that the snow will keep people from coming to the ball."

"Oh, are more coming in? I assumed it was just the Pendolphin House guests who were attending." Warren aimed the SUV down the house's long driveway, heading for Port Willis.

"Yes, there are about fifty more donors coming tomorrow, mostly from London. Pendolphin House wasn't large enough to host everyone overnight, so I helped them find lodging in Port Willis and surrounding villages." She shrugged. "I thought it might make it more exclusive if only 'premier donors'—those willing to give the most—could stay at the house."

Warren chuckled as they drove down the empty country road, a velvety blanket of stars tossed over the sky above them. "For someone who doesn't believe she belongs among the wealthy, you sure seem to understand what motivates them."

Them. Interesting. Warren didn't seem to lump himself into the same category.

"How are you doing?" His tone had turned soft, concerned.

"Um, great. Everything is set for the ball. It'll be a busy day tomorrow, but nothing I can't handle."

"That's wonderful." A pause. "But it's not what I was asking."

She sighed. "I know." He meant after last night—after the nightmare. "I was able to go back to sleep when I returned to my room, so that was huge."

"I'm glad." Now that the vehicle was toasty, he turned the knob down just a tad. "You said you get the nightmares more than you'd like?"

"Yes." She grew quiet, her focus on the lights in the distance—the village of Port Willis, all lit up and ready for a fun night. Her guests were there, likely throwing money around and having a grand old time. How she wished she could be as carefree as all of them.

Not with money, but life in general. If she could only let go of the past the way they let go of their credit cards …

Kara closed her eyes and set her head back against the seat. "The nightmares started after I left Jeff. Over and over, I dream that Rose will be taken away from me. Jeff is always there. Sometimes he's looming larger than life. Sometimes he's just his normal self, but stronger, tougher somehow." A tear slid down her cheek. "But always, he's laughing at me, because he knows."

"What does he know?"

Kara swallowed hard and opened her eyes, studying Warren's profile in the moonlight as he watched the road. "That I'm weak. That I can't do this. Can't support my daughter on my own."

"Kara, you're one of the strongest women I know."

"You must not know very many then." She tried a chuckle, but it came out a croak. "I can't even move out of my sister's house, Warren. We've been there three whole years. I have the money. It's not that. I just can't seem to make myself do it, because I'm worried. Like, what if I pick the wrong house? Or I wake up in the middle of the night with a nightmare, and another adult isn't there to talk me down? What if I scar my daughter for life?"

"Not that those aren't valid fears, but are they really what you're worried about?"

"I don't know. Maybe not. I want more than anything to show the world that I can do this. That I can stand on my own two feet without falling on my face." She was quiet for a few moments. "The only thing I know for sure is that my poor sister deserves to have her life back without the burden of constantly helping me."

Silence reigned between them as they entered the town and Warren navigated the crowded streets. Finally, he found a parking lot at the top of the hill and maneuvered the SUV between two Smart cars. When he placed the car into Park, he unclipped his seatbelt and turned to face her. "Kara, I'm willing to bet that your sister does not think of you as a burden."

"She'd never say that. Wouldn't even think it. But—"

"But nothing." Warren reached across the console and took her hand. "While I think it's noble that you want to prove you can stand on your own two feet, it's not weakness to depend on other people. We aren't meant to do life alone."

Kara stared at their connected hands. His words penetrated her heart, and she wanted nothing more than to lean into the solace he was offering to her.

Oh, how she wanted to believe him. To take his hand without worrying about the consequences, the what-ifs.

But in this moment, Fear started shouting again —and she was difficult to ignore.

❄

Kara had never seen the streets of Port Willis so full.

Together, she and Warren climbed from the vehicle and followed the flow of people from the parking lot down the hill toward the park where she had first glimpsed Warren in town. There must be several hundred villagers and tourists alike crammed onto the grassy bluff, waiting for the large tree to be lit.

The night sky was perfect for it—clear and crisp. Kara could see her breath in the air as she and Warren ambled toward the gazebo, where several long tables with red and silver tablecloths boasted an assortment of delectable goodies. Ginny and her husband, Sarah and Michael, and a tall gentleman with glasses and curly blond hair—Sophia's husband, William—served guests from behind the tables.

A separate self-serve drink station had been erected on one side, but before Kara could suggest that they grab a cup of cider, a white-haired woman with a microphone climbed the steps of the gazebo with the assistance of a well-dressed, forty-something man with a beard.

The crowd collectively hushed and turned toward her.

"Welcome to our lovely little village of Port Willis." Speaking with a British lilt, the woman was as merry as an elf. "For those who don't know me, I'm Mavis Lincoln, the owner of the local antique shop just up the road. My handsome escort here is my nephew, Oliver. Sorry, ladies, he's taken."

Oliver—oh, Joy's husband! Kara searched the crowd for her friend, who—despite her short stature —stood out like a red dress at a black-and-white ball in her bright yellow jacket and hot pink pants. Joy blew Oliver a kiss from her spot beside raven-haired Sophia, who was holding her son on her hip and trying to keep young Emily from snatching another cookie from the sweets table.

Kara giggled at the sight. The girl reminded her so much of Rose at that age.

Oh, Rose.

Just twelve more days and she'd get to hold her daughter in her arms again. Safe. Together.

Mavis continued. "Thank you for coming to our third annual Port Willis Winter Walk. We hope you'll stick around town and shop to your heart's content until nine o'clock. But first, let us get this tree lit, shall we?"

The crowd cheered, and Warren stepped closer

to Kara. Had he meant to or was it simply the jostling crowd that had caused his sudden proximity? Either way, she didn't hate the way their arms now pressed against each other, leaving her whole body warm despite the cold outside.

Different smells swirled in the air—from chocolate to the coming snow—but more than anything, she became aware of the citrusy notes of Warren's cologne as they wrapped around her.

Behind Mavis, Oliver snagged two black electric cords and held them aloft, just inches apart.

"Ten, nine, eight …" Mavis chanted.

The crowd joined in on the countdown, including Kara and Warren, who looked at each other and smiled. And then, just before the lights came on, Warren's gloved hand snuck inside Kara's.

But this was different than the way he'd held her hand in the car—all comfort and friendship.

This time, he intertwined their fingers. And despite the layers of fabric between their skin, it was hard to ignore the way his thumb stroked hers.

The group surrounding them oohed and aahed with delight as the tree came alive before their eyes. The explosion of white light matched Kara's insides as the warm glow burst forth.

How had this happened? One minute, she'd been so determined to remain single forever. The next, Warren had taken down her defenses with his sweet ways and to-die-for smile.

And she'd given in.

Was it weakness? Or was it true strength?

"We aren't meant to do life alone."

The thought curled and twisted—and settled—as Kara's eyes took in the splendor before her.

When the cheers died down, Mavis spoke again. "Now, before I release you to shop till you drop, as my American friends would say, please enjoy our local handbell team's rendition of a holiday favorite."

Kara hadn't even noticed, but just to the left of the tree, a group of fifteen or twenty had gathered behind four or five long lined tables. Each person held two bells with more on the table in front of them. On their conductor's signal, they began to play, and the sweet melody of "Silver Bells" lifted over the crowd.

Some audience members quietly dispersed, while others snuggled together and listened to the music twining up, up, up into the air. When the group had finished, Kara reluctantly pulled her hand from Warren's to offer a polite clap. "That was lovely."

"It really was." Warren eyed her for a moment and then tucked his hands into his pockets. Oh no. Had he thought she didn't want to hold his hand anymore? "Want to snag a cider?"

"S-sure." With his absence from her side and the continually dropping temperature, her teeth had started to chatter. She could use a hot drink to warm her up.

Making their way toward the drink station, they joined the line for cider. Kara racked her brain for something to say. "I've never heard a handbell choir before, have you?"

"Actually, I have. My mother is obsessed with them."

"Really?" Kara huffed out a laugh as they moved forward a few inches in line. "Why?"

"She grew up in a small town in Connecticut. I guess bells were a really huge deal there, at the holidays and all year round. The local church on the square rang them at every birth, every death. And of course at Christmas, to symbolize Christ's birth too." Warren kicked at a blade of grass under his boots. "My mom loved them so much that as a teen, she ran around town convincing people to restart the local handbell choir, which had fizzled out years before that."

"Wow." Kara knew Warren's mom from a distance—they'd been on a few charity committees together when Kara had been married to Jeff—and had a hard time picturing her as a carefree young woman who was passionate about handbells, of all things. "Does she still play?"

He shook his head. "Not since my grandpa died. I think a lot of her love for them stemmed from him."

"Why is that?" They'd almost reached the front of the line. Kara could smell the spiced apple drink and couldn't wait to taste it.

A flicker of a smile crossed Warren's lips. "My grandpa was quite a character. Mom told me how he used to carry around a silver bell—all the time, not just at the holidays—and ring it whenever something made him happy."

"Did he ring it a lot?"

"Yeah, I guess he did." Warren coughed. "He died when I was a kid, so I don't remember much about him. In fact, that bell actually sat on our mantel for a long time and I didn't know what it was. But when my mom reminded me of the bell and what it had meant to my grandpa, then I recalled him ringing it. And I asked her if I could have it."

Now at the front of the line, Kara reached for a cup and handed it to Warren. "Did she give it to you?"

"She did." He took the cup from her. "I try to take it with me whenever I travel. Just a little piece of home, you know?"

Grabbing another cup, she held it under the dispenser's spigot and pressed on the handle. Steaming light brown liquid flowed into her cup. "And do you ring it like he did when something makes you happy?" She stepped back to allow Warren access to the dispenser.

He quieted for a moment, filling his cup, the din of the crowd bustling and swirling around them. When his cup was full, he joined her, but didn't take a drink.

Instead, he took her free hand in his and didn't remove his gaze from hers. "I'll admit, I don't always remember to ring the bell."

Her blood thrummed through her veins. The way he was looking at her …

"But if I had it with me right now, I'd be ringing it to the moon and back."

"Warren …" That was all she could say because he —his presence—turned her brain into mush.

"Kara, I don't know how you feel, but I like you. A lot."

Sweet apple cider, kill her now. "I don't …" She trailed off, looked away.

"It's okay if you don't feel the same way." His voice didn't communicate hurt. Instead, it remained strong, but tender. "That won't change how much I like and respect you. But I *will* back off if you don't feel the same way."

Her gaze collided with his once more. "It's not that. I … I do. Like you, that is." Had she really just admitted that to his face? *Oh my.* "I'm just not sure if I'm ready. Jeff …"

"I know." Warren squeezed her hand. "And that's okay too. There's no pressure here. I just wanted you to know where I stand."

From several feet away, someone called to them.

Kara glanced over and saw Sarah and Michael waving them over to their horde of friends. Quickly, she dropped Warren's hand. It was one thing to consider dating again, but another for others to observe it. That would somehow make it more real. "I'll think about what you said, okay?"

"Take all the time you need. I'm not going anywhere." He angled his head toward the group. "I guess we've got some mingling to do, huh?"

"Let's do it," she said in a teasing voice as she mimicked his enthusiastic reply from earlier this evening.

He laughed and they walked toward Sarah and the rest of the gang. Their "date" may have been over, but who knew what the rest of her trip might hold?

So much of it depended on Kara—on her ability to let go of the past and embrace the possibilities of the future.

But that required trust.

And she just didn't know if she could get there, however much she wanted to.

CHAPTER 8

*E*verything was perfect.

Kara glanced around Pendolphin House's ballroom, a pure vision of wonder and wintry delight. Shimmery blue curtains hung as backdrops along the walls, and soft snowflakes had been spotlighted on the dance floor. On the far end, near the stage where the musicians would play, three Christmas trees of varying heights had been arranged, iridescent "snow" flocking their branches.

Guests would begin arriving in an hour, where they'd dance for a bit, then join together in the dining room for dinner and a guest speaker—a woman Sarah personally knew who had once been in an abusive relationship but had become one of London's loudest advocates for battered women and children. After that, the evening would continue with dancing until the wee hours of the morning.

Windows lined the upper third of the ballroom walls, showcasing the brilliant nighttime starry jewels in the sky, a full moon, and wisps of clouds that were carrying snowflakes. The snow had begun to fall last night in London, and the storm was making its way to Port Willis as Kara and the others —caterers, florists, musicians, and more—bustled around Pendolphin House preparing for the ball.

Clasping her clipboard, Kara reviewed her checklist one final time. Check, check, check.

It was done. All had gone seamlessly. She could hardly believe it.

It was too good to be true.

"Kara!" Sarah's voice rang out above the squeaks and squawks of the string quartet tuning their instruments on the raised platform in the corner of the massive ballroom. She dodged staff members as she made her way over in a dark green ball gown that hugged her baby bump. Hair curled and swept to the side with a diamond pin, Sarah looked every inch the socialite she'd been raised to be.

"Sarah, you look so beautiful." Kara embraced her boss—who, in the last few days, had become even more a friend. "Has Michael seen you yet? If not, be prepared for him to be speechless."

Sarah laughed as she pulled back from Kara's embrace. "My husband? Speechless? Please." She took in Kara, with her floor-length dress in a deep Christmas red. "And I'm not the only one who looks beautiful. Kara! Wow. Warren isn't going to know what hit him either."

"Oh, well." Kara looked away, biting her lip. It's not as if she and Sarah had even spoken about Warren again after that night in the bakery, but maybe she'd seen the way Kara hadn't wanted to leave his side last night at the tree lighting. She had to admit, if Warren hadn't been here, she might not have taken such care with her appearance tonight. But when Gwen had offered to fix her hair in a lovely updo, she hadn't been able to resist.

She let her fingers glide over the beaded bodice of her dress. "You don't think it's too much?" Kara had planned on a years-old black dress she'd worn to countless functions, but then Cindy had bought her this one. Her sister had been shopping at her favorite consignment shop in Boston when she'd found the off-the-shoulder gown with a tulle skirt that shimmered when it caught the light.

But though Kara had protested the purchase at first, she had to admit … when paired with a faux-diamond drop necklace and earrings, the dress kind of made her feel like a princess at the ball.

Now all she needed was her Prince Charming.

But was she really ready? She'd told Warren she wasn't sure, but a late-night gab session with her sister when she'd returned last night had bolstered her confidence.

"You will never be able to guarantee anything in this

life, Kara. The best you can do is pray, ask for guidance, look for red flags, and dive in. No toe dipping. Dive."

Now, Sarah returned her to reality with a gentle touch to Kara's elbow. "It's definitely not too much." She tucked her bottom lip under her teeth. "So. Not to change the subject, but I have a huge favor to ask."

Her tone of voice made the hair prickle on the back of Kara's neck. "Okay. What's up?"

"I just spoke with our guest speaker, Linda. Turns out, thanks to the weather, she got into a car accident on the way down here." Sarah waved her hands in the air. "Nothing serious, but her tires are flat and she's still a few hours away. We need to find a Plan B for our dinnertime talk."

Kara began to pace. This wasn't good. "We were counting on Linda's talk to bring in extra donations —donations that we desperately need as we open the London branch."

"I know."

"And I didn't have a Plan B for that." For flowers? Appetizers? Musicians? Yes. Those could all be replaced easily. But a guest who could speak to the atrocities that battered women faced every day? One who might move attendees enough to encourage them to open their wallets even more?

What were they going to do?

"I have an idea." Sarah's voice was guarded, hesitant.

And when Kara glanced up at her boss, she knew

why. She held up her hands and shook her head. "What? Me?"

"Yes. You."

"Oh no. I … I can't."

Sarah snagged both of Kara's hands, holding them fast. "Kara, I know what I'm asking is a lot. But there's no one better qualified to speak about this than you."

"I …" Kara squeezed Sarah's hands harder than she'd squeezed those of the nurse who had been at her bedside when Rose was born. How could she go on that stage and tell the world what Jeff had done to her? Not even Sarah knew the particulars. Not all of them.

And Warren—he'd never look at her the same way again.

Oh sure, they knew in theory that Jeff had beaten her. Manipulated her.

But if she described the depths of his depravity—and then talked about how long she'd let him treat her like that?

It would be mortifying.

Because even though her therapist had talked her through the shame, it still lurked. And right now, it was choosing to rear its ugly head.

Bearing the shame inside herself was one thing, but to show it off to the world—or at least, a roomful of people who hadn't lived what she had lived? To confess that she'd been a victim because she hadn't been strong enough to stand up for herself the very first time Jeff had smacked her?

But what other choice did they have? New Dawn needed this—needed her to step up.

Kara had always said she'd do anything to further the mission. She'd just never expected this.

Still …

"I'll do it."

"Really? Are you sure?"

No. "Yes, of course. Whatever it takes, right?"

"Well—"

"Excuse me. I've got to go … think."

Before Sarah could say more, Kara raced down the long wooden ballroom and out into the hallway, down the stairs, and out a side entrance that led to the vast gardens. The chill in the air made her gasp, but that didn't stop her from clomping down the pathway in her heels, following its twists and turns until she ended up next to a large tree near the edge of the bluff.

The dark ocean tumbled and crashed on the rocks below, signifying everything she felt inside.

Her chin trembled and her eyes burned. She tried to hold back the tears—she'd spent way too long on her makeup to let her mascara run—but eventually lost the battle.

Placing a closed fist at her stomach, Kara leaned against the tree and allowed the tears to fall. She cried and cried, losing track of time, the wetness stinging her now freezing cheeks. A guttural moan left her lips, and she was grateful no one was around to see her completely fall apart. Her legs shook and nearly gave way.

But just when she was about to collapse, strong arms came around her waist, supporting her.

And she knew who was holding her even before she turned around and tucked her arms inside the warmth of his black Armani tux jacket.

How had he even found her all the way out here?

"Shh." Warren rubbed circles on her back as she cried. "It's okay. You're not alone, Kara."

That nearly had her crying even harder, but eventually, her body shuddered and the tears stopped. She needed to get back to the ball—back to her job—but Kara allowed herself to enjoy Warren's embrace just a bit longer before pulling back and running her hands down the front of her dress. "I'm sorry."

The clouds above them threatened to dump their quarry at any moment. The smell of snow was imminent.

"You don't have to be sorry." Warren pulled a handkerchief from his pocket and gave it a shake. "May I?"

She must look terrible—all the time she'd taken on her appearance, wasted. Thanks to the partially blocked moon, perhaps Warren couldn't see the disastrous details, but there were lampposts along the pathway and one not too far away that might be giving him a full view of Kara in all her post-cry glory.

Nevertheless, she nodded.

Slowly, as if not to spook her, he lifted the cloth to her face and dabbed first her cheeks, then underneath her eyes. Even in the dim lighting, his intense focus and drawn lips showed that he was a man on a mission.

Finally, he stepped back, tilting his head and lowering the handkerchief. "Beautiful."

At that, Kara couldn't help but snort. "Liar."

But he didn't crack even a smile. Warren closed the distance between them once more, placed one hand around her waist, and raised his other to trace her cheekbones. "I'm not lying. Kara, you are never more beautiful than when you're showing off your true self."

Oh, this man. "How did you find me?"

"I saw Sarah right after you'd left and she pointed me in your direction. She thought she might have upset you."

Kara shook her head. The moonlight cracked through a few clouds, just for a moment, then mostly disappeared again. "*She* didn't upset me so much as her request."

Warren's hand flexed at her waist. "What request?"

Breathing deep, she informed him about Linda being a no-show. "And she wants me to fill in."

"But?" Warren studied her, and for the first time she took in the full effect of him all dressed up for the evening. His tux hugged his shoulders, making them appear even broader than she remembered, and his hair seemed to have a bit of extra wave to it tonight. Gone was the five o'clock shadow he'd sported more than once while here. While she kind of missed it, her fingers itched to run along the now-smooth skin of his jaw.

"Kara?"

Her cheeks warmed. She hadn't meant to stare.

"But I don't have any clue what to say. I've never told my story publicly." Kara sighed. "My therapist and my sister are the only ones who know everything."

"No one is asking you to give every detail." He tucked an errant hair behind her ear, his touch so sweet, so gentle, that she leaned into it. "And if you don't feel comfortable, then we will think of something else. It's not up to you alone to save the organization. We're a team."

That was true. There had to be other options—what, she didn't know, but surely they could put their minds together and come up with something.

"But…"

Her nose scrunched. "What?"

"But I think there would be value in telling your

story. Not for anyone else's sake. Not even for New Dawn. But for yourself."

"I just don't want people to see me like that, you know? As a victim." Needing something to do with her hands, she fiddled with the top button of his jacket.

"What people? There are only a handful of people in that audience that even know you—and just a few you might call friends. Who cares what they think?"

"Okay." She lifted her chin. "I don't want *you* to see me that way. Like I'm … weak." Her voice strained as she turned from him and walked to the edge of the bluff. Wind blew at her skirt and hair, whipping them into who knew what kind of shape. All of Gwen's work unraveled around her shoulders.

Kara ran her hands up and down her upper arms. If she didn't return to the house soon, she'd become an icicle. But she couldn't quite face the task in front of her. Not yet.

She'd given him a chance to slink away, but no, there Warren came, beside her once more. Before she knew it, he'd placed his jacket over her shoulders, encasing her in warmth. "I've already told you what I think—you're not weak. You're strong, Kara. You left one of the most powerful men in Boston. That took guts."

"I tell myself that, but the lies sometimes are so strong. And I'm tired of fighting them."

"My grandma used to say that lies lose their

power when exposed to the light. I'm not a therapist, but I do think there's power in telling your story. And maybe some of that fear, that shame, that you still feel will lose its potency if you speak it out loud."

"Maybe you're right."

They stood there together for a few moments in silence.

Then, "Kara, I don't know what it's like to be you. No one has lived your life, and no one has the right to judge you for any part of it. We all have our demons."

"Even you?"

He laughed. "Are you kidding? Definitely me."

"Prince Charming has demons? I've got to hear this."

"Prince Charming, huh? I like that." Warren hip bumped her. "Who does that make you?"

She tapped her chin with her pointer finger. "I'm still figuring that one out."

"Let me know when you do?" And there was something so unguarded—wistful—about the way he asked that she took his hand and squeezed.

"You'll be the first one I come to." She smiled, then squinted up at him. "Seriously, though. What demons?"

Warren rubbed his jaw, then nodded. "I guess I can't really ask you to get up in front of a bunch of people and talk about your painful past if I'm not willing to share mine with you."

"You don't have to." Biting her lip, she reached for his hand. "But I'd like to hear … if you want to tell me." Sure, the tips of her ears and her nose were freezing, but she didn't want this moment to end. Kara had a feeling that he was about to give her a very rare glimpse behind the curtain of who Warren Kensington really was.

He squeezed her fingers and stared across the dark sea below. "About seven years ago, I was engaged."

"Really?" She didn't remember hearing anything about that. Of course, she'd been in the throes of new motherhood, so a lot of society news had evaded her notice. Plus, Warren had lived in New York at the time, hadn't he?

"Yeah. We actually met in grad school, and I liked the fact she didn't come from money. She wasn't like the other women I had dated—well, I didn't think she was anyway."

What did that mean? Kara leaned her cheek against Warren's arm.

Turning his body slightly toward her, he looped his arm around her shoulders and drew her closer. Despite the whoosh of the ocean, she imagined she could hear his heartbeat too. "A few weeks before our wedding, I heard her talking to her mom on the phone—discussing all the ways that marrying me would help her career, all the things she was going to buy once she got access to my money." He cleared his throat. "Her voice, it sounded so … I don't know. Cold. Calculated."

Oh, Warren. "What happened?"

"After I ended the engagement, I graduated with my master's, threw myself into my family's business, and moved to Boston to get away from the memories. But they followed me."

No wonder he'd stayed single for so long. "I'm sorry."

"It's nothing compared with what you've endured."

"One isn't worse than another." Kara's hand slid to his tie, tugging on it so he'd look down at her. "We were both betrayed by people we loved."

"True." Warren's gaze held fast to hers. "It's certainly made me reluctant to date again … until now."

Kara swallowed hard. "Why me, Warren? You don't … you don't know how messed up I am." And after she gave her speech, after he heard the details of what she'd endured, maybe he'd realize just how much baggage she really carried and run for the hills. "Being in a relationship with me would not be easy."

"Easy is relative." He turned and his other arm came around her, enclosing her fully once again. Both of his hands cupped her cheeks, bringing life and warmth to her skin, igniting something inside of her. "I would never worry about *you* wanting me for my money or family connections. That's just not who you are."

"That's certainly true. In fact, I was determined to avoid ever becoming involved again with a man who *had* money and family connections. You know, because of my stepdad. Because of Jeff and the people who protected him." She took a deep breath. "But Warren, you're different. And I'm sorry I ever lumped you into the same category as them."

"I understand why you did."

"Still. I was wrong." She paused. "I can't promise that I won't get scared again, or that I'll be able to trust completely right away." Kara blinked. "But I'm willing to try. With you. That is, if you still feel the same way."

"I do." A pause. "Kara, may I … may I kiss you?"

She froze. But then, the warmth of his hands seeped into her skin and she gave the tiniest of nods.

Warren's lips on hers silenced all her excuses. All her fears. The kiss was short, chaste, and over before she could register it—but it had been nice.

Fine, more than nice.

Much more.

"I hope that answers your question," Warren said. "I *do* still feel the same way, and I don't anticipate that changing anytime soon. If ever."

Okay, then. She smiled. "I like the way you answer questions."

He winked. "There's more where that came

from." Then he snagged her hand. "But right now, we should probably get you inside."

"Oh. Right." The speech. Something sharp twisted in her gut. "Ugh. I'm so nervous."

"I know." He brought her hand to his lips and kissed her fingers, which had begun to go numb from the cold. "But I'll be right there the whole time. I'm not leaving."

Kara only prayed he'd feel the same way once he heard what she had to say.

She was going to be sick, right here, in front of everyone.

Kara stood off to the left of the raised platform where Sarah currently was talking about all of the great things New Dawn had accomplished in Boston. Placing a hand against her stomach, she commanded it to stop roiling like a ship in the middle of a storm. At least there wasn't much in there in case her stomach decided to rebel—between the excited flutter leftover from her kiss with Warren to the panicked butterflies over her impending doom, she'd only taken a few bites of the food she'd so carefully selected for the evening's menu.

As Sarah shared the particulars of a few especially trying cases from the last year, Kara's eyes wandered the dining room. Dozens of round tables had been draped with shimmering silver and blue tablecloths and topped with hurricane vases and gorgeous floral arrangements. Icicle lights strung above the tables gave the effect of melting water frozen in mid-air.

It was all breathtakingly beautiful.

But it was the people that caught Kara's gaze the most. Guests from all over Britain—dressed to the nines in gorgeous reds, silvers, and greens—faced the front, their attention on Sarah.

And soon, on Kara.

Oh, goodness. Was she really going to do this? She was not a public speaker. She was the one behind the events, not the face of them.

God, help.

Now where had that come from? She knew from experience that God didn't answer her prayers.

But maybe she really could use some divine intervention. She was so far outside of her wheelhouse in this moment.

"And now, it's my extreme pleasure to welcome our very own special events coordinator, Kara Gentry, to the stage." Sarah turned toward Kara, arm extended. A smile lit her face, and even from here, Kara saw the clear love and acceptance in her friend's eyes.

With a deep breath and the memory of Warren's encouragement on repeat in her mind, Kara forced her feet to climb the small stage while the audience clapped politely.

Sarah stepped forward and embraced Kara. "You've got this. I'll be right in front if you need a friendly face."

Kara nodded, tight, quick, then released Sarah and moved behind the podium. The applause died down and she swallowed, her hand shaking as she adjusted the short microphone upward just a tad. "Thank you, Sarah." Oh man, her voice sounded like she'd been smoking her whole life. She attempted to clear the dryness away. "I am not usually one to speak in public. In fact, Sarah just asked me to do this a few hours ago because our wonderful guest speaker had a little fender bender. Thankfully, she's all right. We don't need to worry about her. Although she would have been a great speaker, so I'm sad you'll all miss out on her."

Stop rambling! Less than a minute in and she was already botching this. Her heart rammed against her ribcage as if begging for release. Kara closed her eyes for a brief moment, then peeked out again at the crowd. The lights blinded her, but then her eyes finally adjusted again—and they found the spot they'd been seeking.

Warren sat at one of the front tables, Sarah and Michael beside him—but Kara only had enough room in her gaze for him alone. At the sight of him, her heart rate slowed.

"Lies lose their power when exposed to the light."

Right. This was her chance to tell her story. And maybe, along the way, to sway a few hearts as well.

"I'll be honest. I didn't want to be up here. I didn't want to rehash my story for you all. I didn't want to relive it." She chewed her lip. "But who am I kidding? I relive it every day, when I see my daughter struggling to understand why her parents aren't together anymore. When I wake up in cold sweats after a nightmare." Her gaze stayed steady on Warren, who had leaned forward in his chair. "When I meet a wonderful new man but, because of my past, I struggle with giving him all of my heart."

His hand fisting his tie, he gave her a sad smile, nodded. He understood. He accepted her, faults and fears and all. His reaction bolstered her, giving her the strength to look away from him, to connect her gaze with others' in the crowd.

To keep talking.

"I spent my life hiding who I was. Then I spent it hiding what had happened to me. But I don't want to hide anymore." Her voice shook, but no, she wouldn't stop in embarrassment.

Peace like she'd never known flooded into her heart.

She spoke for several more minutes, telling the crowd about the horrors Jeff had put her through— and the ways she was still dealing with the repercussions of that today.

And with every word, her shoulders straightened. Her head lifted. Her lungs took in new breath.

New life.

Was she making an impact among the crowd? Maybe that didn't matter so much as the fact she was making an impact on … herself.

Still, she wanted to reach them, wanted to implore them to keep giving, keep fighting the evil. "I want to end tonight with an apology. I'm sorry—I misjudged the lot of you."

A rustle went up through the crowd.

Kara tilted her head. "For a long time, I thought that those who had money had it made. That being wealthy was something to aspire to. Then, I lived in your world for a time—and I discovered that it has just as many problems as mine did. But someone quite intelligent reminded me that it doesn't matter how much money you have."

She found Sarah in the crowd. Her friend was nodding along, her cheeks slathered in tears. How could Kara ever have held anything against the wealthy class—assuming all rich people were the same—when this woman had fought her own father in order to help Kara? And then there was Warren, a man who had done nothing but show her kindness and encourage her.

"He told me that what counts is what's on the inside, that it's what we do with what we've been given that matters most." Her gaze swept the crowd, which seemed to lean forward collectively as she pressed her speech toward its final moments. "It was because of my own strength—and the support of those around me—that I was able to leave my ex-husband. But it was people like you who gave me the resources to keep my daughter, to keep standing, and to keep fighting. You see, it's a partnership. One cannot exist without the other. You are an integral part in the cycle, and I'm so very grateful for each one of you. Thank you."

As Kara swiped the tears from underneath her eyes and swiveled to exit the stage, the crowd erupted into applause—this time not polite, but strong. Exuberant.

And then, they did something she never expected.

They stood.

They were standing to show their support—but more than that, they were standing *with* her.

Kara pressed her face into her hands, soaking in the applause, the love, the support.

It was too much.

Arms and the scent of lavender surrounded her. Sarah whispered in her ear once more, her voice ragged, "Well done, Kara. Well done." With a squeeze, she let go and hurried up onto the stage. "Thank you so much for that moving speech, Kara. I think what just happened was what some might call a divine appointment. I know I needed to hear it."

There was that word again. *Divine.*

And so maybe, just maybe, God was standing with her too.

Kara walked on wobbly legs back to her seat, but when she reached it, Warren wasn't where he'd been. She looked around the room, where the guests had started to retake their seats, and caught a glimpse of him standing in the back corner, his eyes on her.

Did he want her to join him?

"Someday, you're going to have to learn to trust men again." Cindy's voice popped into her mind. That conversation seemed so long ago, even though it had just been a little over a week.

But sometime between then and right now, a miracle had occurred.

She'd never thought she would trust a man again —but she trusted Warren. Was she a fool, or was this a gift?

Stop second-guessing everything and trust yourself.

Okay, then. Kara snatched a handful of her dress and lifted it so she could walk more quickly and bustled toward the back doors. Warren had moved into the hallway and she followed him to where he studied a painting of a huge oak tree. The wind blew the leaves, some of which tumbled to the ground and every which way—but roots sprouted underneath the soil, digging deep into the earth, holding the tree firm despite the buffeting winds.

That could be her. She wanted that to be her. But

she didn't have to do it alone. And the man in front of her just might have a role to play in making that happen.

The sound of Sarah speaking into the microphone faded as Kara approached Warren from behind. She stopped, her heels sinking into the plush rug beneath her feet as she waited for him to turn. What had he thought of her speech?

Finally, he must have sensed her presence, because he pivoted. "Kara." He spoke her name with such reverence, such adoration, that she couldn't do anything but step forward into his arms. Warren hugged her close, his nose sinking into her hair. "You were …"

The close press of his body against hers, his arms surrounding her, his warm breath on her neck—they all made her shiver in a new and thrilling way. "I was …?"

"Brilliant."

She pulled back. "Yeah?"

"More than yeah."

That tugged a grin across her lips. "Did you like the part where I quoted you?"

"You quoted me? I hardly noticed." But his returning smile showcased his teasing. "Seriously, Kara. I am very sorry for all that man put you through. I wish …" He swallowed, his Adam's apple bobbing.

"I know. Me too." Kara studied the contours of

his face—his cheeks, his brow … his lips. "That's my past, and while it will probably continue to haunt me in certain ways, I don't want it to define who I am anymore. I am not a victim. I'm a survivor."

"And an amazing one at that."

She stared at him for three, two, one, and then she couldn't stand it anymore. She needed to kiss this man. And not some two-second buss on the lips either. Kara wanted to get lost in him, in this magic and connection pulsing between them.

So, lifting up on her tiptoes, she brushed a kiss against his lips. Then, with eyes closed, she wrapped her arms around Warren's neck. He caught her around the waist, one hand on her hip, one in her hair, and kissed her back with the power of all they'd been holding back.

Together, their mouths moved in a dance that, somehow, they both seemed to know. A heady fog consumed her.

So this was what she'd been missing. What she'd almost missed, because of fear.

Pulling back slightly, Kara let loose a sigh. "Wow."

"You've got that right." He seemed a bit dazed as he played with one of her earrings, brushing his fingers against the side of her neck.

Mmm. Not sure she would ever tire of this— whatever this was. And because he'd been quite the gentleman, leaving the ball in her court, it was up to her to clarify. "So … what now?"

Somehow, he understood her question that wasn't really a complete thought. "Now, we go back in and dance the night away. And then, I'm taking you on a proper date on Monday night. How does that sound, Snow?"

Her brow scrunched. "Snow?"

"As in Snow White? I mean, if I'm Prince Charming ..." He shrugged, and they both laughed. "Besides, it seems only appropriate, given the weather at the moment." Warren nodded at the window a few feet away.

There, against the dark night, snowflakes fluttered from the sky. The snowfall wasn't heavy or rushed. It was almost tender in its descent, allowing an invisible hand to move it to and fro until it landed below.

"Hmm. Snow. I like it." She kissed him once more for good measure. "And I would like nothing more than to go out with you on Monday, my prince."

CHAPTER 9

$\mathcal{K}$ara hadn't known the Port Willis crowd long, but she already felt like she belonged more among them than she ever had among the wealthy set.

Though, as she was learning, perhaps it was less about wealth and more about allowing herself to be … well, herself.

And here, tucked into a booth at the Village Pub —Michael's family restaurant where they'd eaten on her first day in town—with a handful of women, Kara was finally ready to be open. Vulnerable.

Because she majorly needed some advice.

Clearing her throat, Kara flicked a finger down the moisture gathering on the outside of her water glass. "I was wondering if I could ask you ladies a question."

The conversation around the table halted and

Kara found four sets of eyes focused on her. When Sarah had suggested a girls' night after the last Pendolphin House guest had left this morning, Kara had been on too big a high—from the massive success of the fundraiser to her upcoming date with Warren and, yes, THOSE KISSES—to say no.

But over the last few hours, doubt had wriggled in. She'd dialed Jeff's phone five times in a sudden and desperate attempt to talk to Rose, her grounding point, but of course they must already be on their ship, which was set to sail tonight.

So … yes. Advice.

Sarah dragged a fork through her mashed potatoes. "Well, don't leave us all in suspense," she teased. Behind her, a collection of pastel-painted seashells decorated the wall. In fact, the entire restaurant consisted of vintage oceanside decor. That, along with the cozy fireplaces and the wooden beams spaced along the ceiling, created the perfect environment for this conversation. "What's the question?"

Where to begin? "Well … um." Kara's legs fidgeted under the table and the seat of the booth groaned a bit as she shifted. "I kind of have a date tomorrow night—"

"I knew it!" Ginny pumped her fist in the air. Beside her, a smiling Sophia rolled her eyes and gave her friend a little shove.

Joy grinned at Kara from across the table. "Warren's a lucky guy."

Kara shook her head, smiling. "How did you know it was with Warren?"

"Oh, please." Ginny snapped. "The two of you are as obvious a pairing as pasta and cheese, as salted caramel and chocolate, as—"

"We get the picture, sister dearest." Sarah laughed, then turned back to Kara. "I'm really happy to hear that. I've thought for a few years now that you two would make a cute couple. Of course, I knew you had a lot to work through first."

"That's the problem. I still feel like I do." Kara nibbled the edge of her crusty roll before continuing. "And I can't help but wonder if I'm making a mistake. I don't want to be this wishy-washy person. I want to trust him. I do trust him. But …"

"But it's hard to forgive and trust *yourself*." Sophia's words were soft, so quiet that Kara had to strain to hear her, which was strange, since they were some of the only patrons here this late on a Sunday evening.

"Yes, exactly." Kara cocked her head. "How did you know?"

The other women eyed each other, as if they knew a secret Kara didn't. But before she could slink back into herself, sure she'd never really be part of the group, Sophia spoke again. "Before William, I was engaged to a man who emotionally abused me. And I was a domestic violence therapist, of all things. If anyone should have 'known better,' it was me."

Whoa. Kara sat back, the slats of the upper booth hard on her shoulders. "I'm so sorry." With her pause came a charged electricity in the air. "How … how did you learn to trust again, if you don't mind me asking?"

"Of course I don't mind." Sophia fiddled with her long silver necklace, which perfectly matched her stylish soft sweater. "It took time, but eventually William proved to me that he was nothing like David. And God proved to me that he'd been there with me all along, despite the fact I had dismissed his help for so long."

"I'm not sure he's very interested in my situation." Kara tried for a laugh, but it fell flat. "Or me." Then again, her speech *had* gone really well last night. But was that because of him, and her desperate last-minute prayer, or would she have been fine on her own all along?

"I thought that too." Giving her an understanding smile, Sophia nodded. "But ultimately, the abuse was David's fault and no one else's. So, even though God's protection didn't look exactly the way I thought it would—or should—it was still there. *He* was there."

A shiver raced along Kara's arms. Maybe she'd have to think on that one a bit more. "Just hearing from you that it's possible to move forward and have a healthy relationship after such a hard past gives me hope."

"Oh, girl," Ginny chimed in. "All of us here have had to overcome something difficult in our past before we were able to find the loves of our lives. Not saying Warren is that for you, but it's awesome that you're willing to try again. That's seriously the first step."

"Yes, you should be really proud of yourself, Kara." Sarah reached over and squeezed her hand.

"I am." And that speech yesterday had given her a freedom she hadn't expected—even though Warren had predicted it.

But back to what Ginny had said. "You mentioned that you each had to overcome something?" Were these women willing to open up to her, somewhat a stranger? If they could do that, surely she could find the courage to do the same.

At her question, Joy gave an effusive nod. "Oliver dropped into my lap when I wasn't even looking for him. Like you, I'd kind of decided I was good being single forever. And then, when I did meet him—and fell hard—I didn't think I could keep him because I was so busy taking care of my mother." She shrugged. "It all worked out in the end, once I was willing to recognize that God wanted to bless me with wonderful things—if I was open to them."

Kara was certainly sensing a theme. Was God at

the center of each woman's story? And what did that mean for her?

She turned to Sarah. "What about you?" Kara knew the basic story of how her boss had met Michael, how he'd followed her home to Boston after her month-long stay in Port Willis several Christmases ago, but nothing of a hardship.

Pursing her lips, Sarah furrowed her brow. Then she dove into the story of fighting her dad for control of her own life and assuming that she and Michael didn't have a future because it didn't fit into her plans—or the ones her parents had for her life. "I got so wrapped up in what I thought I should do for everyone else's sake that I didn't stop to consider Michael was a wonderful gift I hadn't asked for." A pause. "I know you're probably hesitant to date again because of Rose, but consider who you want to be in charge of your life—Fear or Hope."

Fear had been Kara's companion for too long. How she longed to break free of its grasp once and for all. Maybe going on a date with Warren tomorrow was the first step.

No, the first step had been leaving Jeff. Then fighting for Rose. Then working for New Dawn.

And telling her story last night.

Every step she'd taken—large or small—had accumulated, like a snowball rolling downhill. Together, they had tipped the scales toward Hope, unbalancing Fear and removing it from the throne Kara had allowed it to take in her life.

She just couldn't allow Fear to take over once more. And being honest about her struggles was a big part of that. "I'm inspired by all of your stories. I just … I'm so afraid of failing again, you know?"

"I totally get that," Ginny said. "After my first husband left me, all I could dwell on was my failures."

"So how did you overcome that?"

"I'm not saying I don't still struggle with it, because there are times I do." Ginny glanced around the table at each of the women, who nodded in turn —like some sort of solidarity linking them, rising between them.

Here was a group of women who had fought their pasts … and won.

Kara wanted more than anything to be like them.

"But," Ginny continued, "it turns out that my past didn't make me a failure. The things I've been through helped to shape me into who I am now, and I had a choice—I could either wallow in those low points or I could use them to help others and learn from my mistakes. I could either take on the label of Failure or find my value in the fact that God loves me no matter what I do or don't do. He loves me simply because I'm his."

It wasn't the words—though those were powerful

too—but the peace radiating from Ginny's eyes that seared Kara in the gut.

She wanted that.

And, she realized with a start, she'd had it … during her speech. The peace had been other-worldly. But now, it was gone again. Maybe in order to make it a permanent fixture in her life, she'd have to figure out where she stood with God.

Kara was just learning to trust herself and men again. Learning to trust God too? That might be too tall an order at the moment.

There was definitely a lot to think about—but first and foremost, and most pressing, her date tomorrow night.

"Thank you for sharing all of that, ladies. I really appreciate your insights." She took a sip of water and smiled. "Now, for somewhat of a lighter subject—got any tips for going on my first first date in forever?"

CHAPTER 10

Had it really been three days since she'd officially gone out with Warren for the first time?

Since he'd picked her up from her room at Rebecca's B&B—where they were both guests again, although not the only ones—and taken her to a small Italian-inspired restaurant in town where they'd talked until the place closed …

Since, despite the cold snap and snow, they'd walked hand in hand along the bluff overlooking the Port Willis harbor quay and talked about her passion for New Dawn and his passion for charities involving work in third-world countries …

Since they'd returned to the bed and breakfast and eaten Rebecca's pie in front of the fireplace until two in the morning …

Since he'd walked her back to her room and given her another spine-tingling kiss …

Now, two days before Christmas, Kara hung up after a brief call with her daughter—heart full and at peace. Rose was having a wonderful time on the cruise going to the children's club every day. Despite their distance, at least Kara had been able to consistently talk with Rose once a day.

The idea of being apart on Christmas still didn't sit well with her, but next year would be different.

In fact, if the last three days spent in constant company with Warren—exploring an old lighthouse just outside of town, taking a driving tour of the surrounding villages and countryside, digging through antiques at Mavis Lincoln's shop, and making cookies together in Rebecca's kitchen—and the intense emotions Kara already felt were any indication, next Christmas could very well be life changing.

A shiver of pleasure coursed through her at the thought just as a knock sounded on her door.

"It's unlocked," she called as she sat up on the bed and smoothed down her hair.

Warren stuck his head in. He had a pizza and some napkins in his hand. "Is your call done?"

"Yep. Come on in."

He hesitated, cocking his head. "Did you want to eat this downstairs?"

"And have Rebecca yell at us for preferring this

over her mince pies?" Kara waved him into the room. "Plus, a large group of loud men checked in earlier today and I'm peopled out."

Chuckling, Warren closed the door behind him and walked toward her, setting the pizza and napkins on the side table. "I completely understand." Then he tugged a chair over from under the window and lowered himself into it.

"Don't want to sit next to me?" she teased.

But instead of an answering smile, a look of desire flashed in his eyes. "Believe me, that's not it."

"Oh." Somewhere downstairs, the sound of muffled laughter carried through the floorboards. "I was just kidding."

"I know. But Kara, I like you a lot. I like what we have right now. And I don't want to do anything to mess this up, including moving too quickly." Warren scratched behind his ear. "Does that make sense?"

Yes, it made perfect sense. Because he respected her, he didn't want to rush their physical relationship—something that had never given Jeff any qualms.

And *this* was just one of the many reasons why she was half in love with Warren already.

Wait. What?

Whoa.

But repeating the sentiment to herself didn't make it any less true. Kara flipped open the pizza box lid and removed a slice, which she placed on a napkin and handed to him. "I like you a lot too. In fact, I was just kind of thinking about what next Christmas might be like if …"

Was she being super forward in admitting that?

"I—" Warren frowned, then pulled his phone from his pocket. His face blanched, turning red before he stuffed the phone back where it had been.

"Everything okay?" Taking a slice for herself, Kara bit into the tomato and cheese mixture. The flaky crust was cooked to perfection.

"Yeah, just a work thing. No big deal." He took a bite of his pizza and chewed, his brow furrowed as he stared at the carpet.

The charged air between them had gone cold, flat.

"Warren? You okay?"

"What?" His eyes darted up. "Oh, yeah. Fine. I'm just tired, I guess. Was up early working."

"And then you spent all day carting me around." She said it with a smile, but once again, he didn't respond in kind.

Her skin prickled. He wasn't … hiding anything from her, right?

No. *People are allowed to have off days, Kara.*

"I understand if you need to go to sleep early tonight," she offered.

"Huh?" Warren blinked. "Oh. No. I'm okay. Right where I want to be." But the frown he made as he snagged another bite of his pizza said differently. He polished off the piece and wiped his mouth. "Now where—"

Grunting, he pulled out his phone again and read an incoming message. Ran his hand down his face and sighed.

Okay, that was it. Something was clearly bothering him. And just like he'd been there for her when she had to give that speech on Saturday night, Kara wanted to be there for him. Standing, she circled the bed and squatted beside his chair, placing a hand on his knee. "Talk to me, Charming. What's going on? How can I help?"

He glanced up from the phone and his expression slackened. "I'm sorry. I'm being terrible company." Then Warren flung his phone onto her bed and tugged Kara onto his lap. "It has nothing to do with you, okay? Nothing you need to worry about."

Nothing you need to worry about. Kara winced. Had he really just used the exact words Jeff used to say when he'd "work" late?

But it was just an unfortunate coincidence. Warren would never betray her or lie to her. He'd said it was merely a work thing, and he was the vice president of a company. Surely there were a lot of fires to put out daily, matters that could be frustrating and easily explain the reaction Warren had had to whatever text or email he'd just received.

Kara looped her arms around the back of Warren's neck and nestled against him. "Okay."

His breathing seemed to even out and she wondered for a moment if he'd fallen asleep. But then his lips connected with her forehead and his hand tightened around her waist. "So … next Christmas."

The air was warm again—and crackling. "Yes?"

"Is it …" He paused, his lips brushing her temple again. "Is it too much for me to admit that I hope we're still together?"

She sat up slightly, pressed her nose lightly against his. "No, it's not."

"Kara … I'm feeling things for you that I didn't think I would ever feel this soon."

She played with the hair at the base of his neck. "Me too, Charming."

"Does that scare you?"

"Surprisingly, no. Because it's you."

And then Warren pressed his lips to hers, long and slow, his kiss full of promises—promises too beautiful to fully grasp. Perhaps Kara's friends had been right. God was giving her an unexpected gift, if she could only open her eyes to see it. To be falling in love so quickly sounded absurd, but Warren wasn't a stranger. She'd known him for years. And Kara was no longer a young girl, easily starstruck by riches and good looks.

She knew what mattered, what counted—and the connection between them was not something that came along every day.

When the kiss grew more fervent, Warren finally pulled back. "I think I'd better say good night before my heart—and my good sense—runs away from me."

Giggling like someone much younger than her thirty-eight years, Kara nodded. "I suppose so. See you in the morning?"

"Unless you're sick of me."

"Hmmm, let me think about that." She popped a kiss on his jaw.

"Snow," he growled, shaking his head and grinning. Then he stood with her still in his arms and set her on her feet. "Have I told you lately that I've got it bad for you?"

"I may have inferred that."

"Good." His voice, low and throaty, did something to her insides. They walked to the door and he leaned down, giving her one more kiss before heading back to his room.

Kara closed the door, sighed, and flopped back onto her bed.

Something vibrated on the mattress next to her. Her hand felt around and found a phone. Oh, shoot. Warren had forgotten it. She grinned. Guess she had an excuse to give him another kiss tonight after all.

But as she sat up, her eyes caught sight of her own name on the screen.

In a text.

From Warren's father.

What in the world?

She really shouldn't snoop, but Warren wouldn't keep secrets from her. And he'd understand—given her past—the need for her to just make sure all was well, right? It wasn't an invasion of privacy if he would willingly tell her if she asked. And if he really hadn't wanted her to see it, he would have locked his phone.

Right?

Kara...

She quieted her inner critic. Because, well … she couldn't go through what she'd experienced before. No more betrayal. No more lies. No more being made to feel worthless.

Her hand shaking, she clicked through to the text.

Dad: *See if your new friend Kara has any insights into her ex. She will be of great use to us as this merger with Gentry moves forward. Great work, son.*

What?

She scrolled up to find a few similar text messages, and her whole body grew hot, her hands clammy. It sounded … but it couldn't be how it sounded.

Because how it sounded was that Warren was just using her. Getting close to her in order to put through some merger between his company and Jeff's.

After all the things she'd told him about her ex-husband, Warren wanted to join forces with the man? Really?

"It has nothing to do with you, okay? Nothing you need to worry about."

On top of it all, he'd lied. Because this had everything to do with her.

Or … Kara inhaled. Maybe she was panicking for nothing. Yes, there had to be a good explanation for this, right? But with the evidence staring her in the face, she didn't know what it could possibly be.

Either way, she wasn't sitting around wondering. Not this time. She leaped off the bed and scurried down the hallway, hesitating only a moment before knocking on his door.

The door swung open. "Kara. Hey."

Ignoring his wide grin and curious expression, she held up his phone. "You left this in my room." Her voice spit at him, the accusation clear.

"Oh, thanks." He tilted his head. "Everything okay?"

"Sure, if you call a text from your father *about me* okay."

The blood drained from his face. He glanced up and down the hallway. "Want to come in so we can talk about this?"

"Oh, am I being too loud for you? Don't want to ruin your sterling reputation." Yikes, fine, that was a dig that maybe he didn't deserve. Jeff always said she got "hysterical" when upset. So maybe she should hear Warren out before employing her shrill voice. "Fine." Stepping past him, she entered his room, which smelled so good—like him—that she immediately fought the urge to run.

But she held her ground. "You got a text from your father after you left."

"And you read it?"

"Don't start with me on that. Maybe I shouldn't have, but after everything Jeff did …"

"I thought we established that I'm nothing like your ex." Warren leaned hard against the wall.

"I didn't think you were. But …"

Maybe you're wrong.

But I have to know.

"Regardless of whether I should have looked at the text or not, I did." Phone still in hand, she crossed her arms over her chest. "Can you please tell me what's going on?"

He studied her for a moment before nodding. "I found out my father is considering a merger with Gentry Pharmaceuticals. Of course, I immediately told him there's no way we can trust a guy like Jeff Gentry. He said he knew that, but there were certain advantages to merging anyway."

Ugh. Business and politics—two things Kara despised. "Why is your dad asking about me?"

"Because he isn't listening to me. He's moving forward with the merger anyway and he wants leverage on Jeff so he can get a better deal or something. I don't know."

He sounded sincere. Still ... "You told me this had nothing to do with me. You lied."

"I didn't ..." But then he tilted his head back against the wall and groaned. "I can see how it looked that way to you. Maybe I shouldn't have said it like that, but I just meant that it was a moot point because I would never go along with it. I would never use you like that. Kara, don't you know how I feel about you?" His voice had grown desperate as he speared her with a look to match. "I'm ... I'm falling in love with you."

If looks could melt a person from their warmth, Kara would be a puddle on the floor. But she couldn't ignore the red flags. Not this time.

If she didn't stand up for herself, if she didn't show her strength now, then she was just the same woman she'd been. A victim.

And that was one thing she'd never be again.

If standing up meant standing alone forever, then so be it.

"Jeff told me that too, once upon a time. But love doesn't lie." Kara shoved the phone into Warren's chest and flounced back to her room, head held high.

It was only once the door was firmly shut—and locked—that she sank down against the wall and cried.

At least she wasn't spending Christmas Eve alone. Sarah and Michael had made sure of that.

Kara forced a smile as she settled against Ginny and Steven's bright yellow couch holding a mug of Ginny's cider and listening to the carolers at the front door, where Ginny, Sarah, and their husbands stood listening. The sun had faded long ago, the moon hidden behind clouds, casting shadows across the tiny Cornish village. Outside, the streetlamps burned dim, granting the whole place a mysterious aura.

But also, a calm.

Which was the exact opposite of the raging river of emotions flooding Kara's whole body.

All day, she'd tried to put off thinking about her fight with Warren. Joy and Sophia had invited her over to bake treats. Little Emily had "helped," and Kara's insides had nearly exploded with missing her own daughter. The magic of Christmas felt empty, destroyed, without Rose here.

Without Warren.

She'd ached to belong somewhere, with someone, and Sarah and company had been very kind to include her this evening in dinner and lovely conversation. But being included didn't mean she belonged.

Once again, she was alone.

The carolers stopped their jaunty tune and Ginny whooped and thanked them, supplying them with cookies she'd baked before closing the door. All four of them returned to the living room, laughing and chattering about some of the youngest carolers and how cute they'd looked in their mittens and knit hats.

Kara smiled, only half listening as her gaze swept the room. The fireplace and mantel, where Ginny and Steven's wedding pictures showed a casual affair set in a green, blooming garden. A modest-sized Christmas tree, decorated beautifully with an array of silver and pink ornaments. The couch, a rocking chair, and a coffee table.

To many, it wouldn't seem like much, but the whole house was like this. Charming. Small, but full.

That's what Kara wanted in a home. She didn't care about the trappings anymore, because trappings really were just that—a trap, something to lure a person in, to make her think she was secure.

When really, she was a captive.

If only Kara could get up the courage to create such a home for herself and Rose. Maybe it would be enough. She'd always thought it would.

But now, there was the *what-if*—because she'd pictured Warren there too.

Warren, who was supposed to come today as well, but had backed out at the last minute.

"Kara?"

She startled, sloshing a bit of cider over the edge of her cup onto the couch. Hissing, she jumped up and set the mug on a coaster on the coffee table. "I'm so sorry. Let me get a towel."

Despite Ginny's protests, she raced into the modern-looking kitchen with granite countertops and a small eat-in table and chairs. Snagging a towel from the oven handle, she wet a corner of it.

When she came back into the room, the men were putting on their jackets.

"Where are you guys going?"

Michael smiled. "Sarah had a craving for old-fashioned lemonade, so we thought we'd run over to Mavis's house and snag some since the stores are closed. She always has some on hand."

"Oh. Okay. Well, in case I'm not here when you return, thanks for letting me join you."

"Of course," Steven said and he covered his red

hair with a beanie. "According to our wives, you're family—and that's good enough for us."

And with that, they ducked out the front door, leaving Kara standing there, dumbstruck and holding the limp towel.

Family.

Her lip trembled as she continued toward Ginny and Sarah, who had taken up residence in the recliner and on the non-stained side of the couch, respectively. "A craving, huh?" Kara looked pointedly at Sarah as she squatted beside the sofa and scrubbed the spot her cider had left behind, praying it wouldn't stain.

"Pregnant women get cravings all the time."

"Yeah, but you don't strike me as the kind of woman who would send her husband out on Christmas Eve to satisfy a craving. Not unless you were up to something." Kara arched an eyebrow at Sarah.

From the recliner, Ginny laughed. "She has you there, big sis."

"Fine." Sarah's fingers made absentminded figure eights on her stomach. "When Warren canceled, he gave some lame excuse about work. But of course I pushed him—"

"You? Pushy? Never." Ginny's eyebrows wagged.

"Hush, you."

Their banter eased some of Kara's own tension. These women *had* become like family, opening their homes and lives to her when they didn't have to. This was a safe place. And she could use some feedback. Cindy would have been willing to give some during their short call earlier today, but Kara hadn't wanted to take her sister away from time with her kids to wail about her misfortunes.

She got off her knees and sat back on the couch, avoiding the wet spot. Grabbing her mug of cider again, she breathed in the sweet apple scent. "Did he tell you what happened?"

"No." Sarah's hands stilled. "Only that he didn't think you'd want him here."

"He was right." And not just because she was upset with him—but also, with herself. And she was embarrassed. Confused.

"So what happened?" Ginny's gentle question floated across the room, as soft as the snow falling outside.

"He betrayed me. Or … I think he did." Kara took a deep sip of her drink before putting it back on the coaster. Then she buried her head in her hands and shook her head. "I might have screwed everything up."

The whole story spilled from her lips. "I just don't know which way is up. Who I can trust and who I can't. I don't even know anymore if I can trust myself."

A hand rubbed her back and Sarah's sweet voice broke through Kara's sorrow. "'When I am afraid, I put my trust in you. In God, whose word I praise, in God I trust; I shall not be afraid.'"

Kara stiffened at the words and she straightened, lips twisted into a frown. "You all talked the other night about God—how he loves you, how he gives you good gifts. But how do you know you can really trust him?"

"He's the only one who will never fail us, Kara. Even the best humans in the world aren't perfect. If you're looking to other people, or even yourself, to be your foundation, it will shake and crumble every time. But God, well, he doesn't change. He is not only a firm foundation—He is the *only* foundation worth building our lives on. And he's always been there, loving you."

The idea of not having to stand on her own, ever again … was glorious. And also, a bit unbelievable. "I just haven't always seen that."

Ginny leaned forward and placed a hand on Kara's knee. "It can be difficult when you're only looking at the bad. But look at all the good in your life—like Rose. New Dawn. Even Warren."

Yes, those were all good things. Still … "I don't want to think about him." Because maybe she *had* been too harsh. But how did she know when to trust and when to run?

"Look, Kara, it sounds to me like Warren messed up by not being completely honest with you," Sarah said. "And it makes total sense that you would have doubts, even compare him to Jeff. But do you honestly, deep in your heart, believe that he and Jeff are anything alike? That they have the same heart and intentions?"

"No." The word came out a squeak. "I just don't want to make the wrong decision again."

"Good thing you don't have to make it alone." Sarah gave her a hug, pulling her close. Then Ginny left her spot on the recliner and pushed her way into the group hug, leaving all three of them laughing.

"We aren't meant to do life alone."

All this time, she'd blamed herself for not being strong enough, not being good enough, not being smart enough. But really, it had been her intense desire to belong to something—to someone—that had driven some of her most desperate acts. From the time she was little, she'd craved security. Identity.

Could it really be true that she could find both of those somewhere she'd never looked before?

Instead of pushing Sarah and Ginny away, Kara allowed herself to be held, to accept the gift of their friendship—and to finally, finally, open her heart to One who had been the giver of all these good things in the first place.

CHAPTER 12

It was almost midnight.

The streets were quiet, the air still. Even the snow flurries had stopped for a time.

Kara walked down High Street toward the park, the gazebo—the tree that she could see lit up even from here. Above her, the clouds had cleared away, bringing starlight and moonshine to rest on her skin.

She'd gone back to her room at Rebecca's a few hours ago, but hadn't been able to sleep—not after the revelations earlier tonight. Her whole body felt lighter, her spirit hopeful and as bright as the tree she approached.

The only thing troubling her was Warren. She'd knocked on his door, eager to mend what she'd broken. To see if they could make things work again. But after a full minute of knocking, Rebecca finally peeked around the corner and told her that Warren had checked out earlier in the day.

He was gone.

Of course, she was bound to see him again in Boston, but she didn't want to wait that long. And what if he decided that dating her—taking a chance on loving her—was too much work?

Then you'll be okay.

The sweet words wafted on a sudden breeze, one that wrapped around her like a hug. Yes, it would sting if she had to say goodbye to Warren, a good man who she could see spending the rest of her life with. But she would survive … and she wouldn't be alone.

The tree now loomed large in front of her. This time, she walked right up to it and touched one of the branches, the spindles cold and stiff. But the lights glowing from inside softened it, taking a thing that was partially dead—it was a cut tree, after all—and granting it new life. Purpose.

Tucking her hands back into the pockets of her coat, Kara stood there for a while, breathing in the scent of pine, of hope. It must be Christmas by now, and even though Rose wouldn't be there this morning to open presents, this may just be the best Christmas Kara had ever experienced.

Because she'd never felt like this before.

Once her nose and lips were near frozen, she sighed. "Goodbye, Mr. Tree. I'll see you tomorrow."

Then Kara turned—and stopped, a gasp on her lips.

Because she wasn't alone. And not just metaphorically speaking, but actually, physically, alone.

A man stood inside the gazebo, watching her.

Warren.

It was like déjà vu as Kara walked toward him, her boots trudging through the snow-littered grass, breath puffing in the air. And when she finally went up the steps, she had to reach out and touch him to be sure he was real. "You're here."

Warren snatched her hand and held it between his own. "And you're freezing. You'd think a woman named Snow would know to wear gloves outside right now."

The affection in his voice—as he said her nickname—almost undid her. "I forgot them at the bed and breakfast and didn't feel like turning around." Her toes curled as he blew into his hands, catching hers in a swirl of warmth. "What are you doing here? I thought you'd left."

He shook his head, where he'd placed a knit cap that covered his hair and the tips of his ears. "I'm staying with Oliver and Joy at Mavis's house until tomorrow. I ... I didn't want to make you uncomfortable by staying at Rebecca's any longer."

"Oh." She took one step closer. "But why are you

here, at the gazebo? Is that just some weird movie-like coincidence?"

He laughed. "No, Rebecca called me. Woke me up from a dead sleep and told me that you'd come knocking on my door, that you'd gone out walking at midnight, and that I'd better get my rear out of bed ASAP if I didn't want to be an idiot."

"Sounds like Rebecca, all right." She scrunched her nose. "I didn't know she heard me leave. And I didn't tell her where I was going."

"I guessed that part." His eyes roved her face. "Kara, I'm so sorry about the whole thing with my dad and the company. I should have just been straight with you, but I thought I could handle it without having to bring you into it at all."

"I appreciate and accept your apology. But I have one too." She closed the final few inches between them and wrapped her arms around his neck. In response, he slid his around her waist. "I completely overreacted. I compared you with Jeff again, and that just wasn't fair. You're a different man with a different heart—and I can see you're nothing alike. I was just afraid. Afraid to let myself fall for you. But fall, I have."

"I've fallen for you, too." He brushed a hair out of her face. "Even though it feels really fast, I'm old enough to know exactly what I want, and that's you, Kara. I've been searching all my life for you. Will you let me give you all the affection and adoration you deserve? I know I'm not perfect, but—"

She held a finger up to his lips. "Charming."

"Sorry, Snow." He turned his head and kissed the palm of her hand. "Am I talking too much?" His face moved closer to hers.

"A little, but it's adorable." She shut her eyes, ready for his kiss—a kiss that didn't come.

Because at that moment, Warren pulled back and reached into the inner pocket of his coat. He pulled out a small silver object, about the size of Kara's palm. It was a bit tarnished, but still in pristine condition.

She squinted in the dark. "A bell?"

"My grandfather's bell, to be exact." Warren held the bell between them and rang it, the chime wending sweet music through the air.

"Does that mean you're happy?"

Warren put the bell back into his jacket and resumed his position fully embracing her. "Happy doesn't begin to describe it. I'm not sure words can."

"Then why don't you find some other way to express yourself?" Kara flashed him an impish grin.

And with a chuckle, Warren bent down and kissed her—proving that sometimes the best gifts really did come when a person least expected them.

And that Love conquered all, in the end.

"Wake up, wake up, wake up!"

Kara groaned and rolled over in bed. "What time is it?"

"Seven in the morning, mommy." Rose shook her shoulders. "That's when you said I was allowed to wake you up. Warren's already got the coffee made for you."

Forcing herself onto an elbow, Kara blinked up at her daughter, who was going through a growth spurt. "He does, does he?"

"Mm-hmm, and even though I've been up for an hour, he reminded me that I had to wait to wake you up. So I've been in my room listening to *Magic Tree House*, but now it's seven and time for presents. Let's go, Mommy, let's go!"

"All right, all right." Kara chuckled, but her whole body was still sluggish from sleep. "I know you're excited." And as the sleep fog cleared from her brain, Kara remembered—she was excited to hand out the presents too.

One in particular.

Rose skipped out the door, yelling toward the kitchen that Mommy was up now and present unwrapping would be starting soon. Kara couldn't help but smile at her youthful enthusiasm, remembering how much she'd enjoyed Christmas mornings herself as a child.

She dragged herself from the bed, pressing cold toes against the wooden floors and shimmying toward her closet to grab her robe. She emerged to find Warren standing in the doorway, looking impossibly handsome in his own fluffy gray robe and flannel pants, eyes sparkling behind his glasses.

He held out a mug of coffee toward her. "Merry Christmas, Snow."

Moving toward him, she gave her husband a quick kiss and took the mug in hand. "Merry Christmas, my prince. You ready for your first Christmas with a daughter?"

"I was born ready." He winked and, laughing, they moved together down the short hallway.

It had only been a year since that magical Christmas in Port Willis, but so much had changed. When they'd returned home, Kara and her sister had gone house hunting, and Kara and Rose had moved into this modest three-bedroom not far from Cindy and Travis.

After only three months of dating, Warren had proposed, and they'd married in July.

Though teasing that she was too old to be a wedding attendant, Cindy had served as Kara's matron of honor, and Sarah and Joy as bridesmaids—though being only two months after the birth of little Judah meant Sarah couldn't join in all of the wedding festivities.

Kara had invited Sophia and Ginny to be bridesmaids as well, but they were too busy with their little ones—Sophia with another little girl on the way and Ginny with her newly adopted toddler, Macy—to make the journey overseas.

Still, the day had been everything Kara could have hoped for, albeit much simpler than Warren's parents had wanted. But they doted on Rose and had softened in their treatment of Warren, and he'd forgiven his father for trying to go behind his back with the Gentry merger, which hadn't ended up happening. Their father-son relationship had actually improved greatly when Warren left the family business and started his own charity organization building wells in Africa.

The sun had only just peeked over the horizon as Kara settled on the couch. The smell of coffee wafted from her mug and her stomach roiled. But that was to be expected, if she remembered correctly from last time. She'd need to switch to decaf now anyway.

Kara set the mug on the side table without taking a sip.

Warren switched on the radio and Kara's favorite Michael Bublé playlist started on low, filling the small living room that reminded Kara so much of Ginny's back in Port Willis. Only here, pictures of her and Warren's wedding day filled the mantel, along with some of her favorite memories of Rose in photo form.

By this time next year, God willing, they'd be adding even more memories.

Speaking of her daughter, Rose was currently kneeling at the tree, sorting presents into piles based on recipient. Rose's and Kara's piles were much larger than Warren's.

But even though his pile was smaller, one present was worth more than them all. She'd wrapped it in tissue paper and placed it in a bag under the tree at midnight, after Warren had gone to bed.

Still, Kara tsked at him. "I thought we weren't going to spend that much this year."

He sat down beside her and flung his arm around her shoulders. "It's my first Christmas with both of my girls." Leaning into her, he nuzzled her neck, and she poked him in the side, giggling. He really was too good to her. He'd even agreed to move into their house instead of buying something larger, even though he could easily afford it. But this was home, and it was exactly as she'd pictured it. Charming and full of love. "I couldn't help but spoil you, Snow."

"Hmm, I guess I'll forgive you then."

"Are you guys going to kiss again?"

Kara snorted as she turned to find Rose standing in front of them, hand on a hip and the other clutching a present. When had she turned into such a little sassy pants? "Come here, you." She snatched her daughter onto her lap and started tickling her. Warren joined along and Rose's shrieks filled the room.

This—this was the gift she'd been waiting for all her life. God had been good to her too.

And to think, there was even more to rejoice over.

Suddenly, Kara couldn't wait any longer.

"Rose, there's a present hidden just behind the tree. Go get it and give it to Warren, please."

Eyes wide, Rose leaped up and obeyed.

While she searched, Warren turned his gaze on her. "Hiding presents from me, are we, Wife?"

"I have to keep the mystery alive." She smiled sweetly. Truth was, their marriage hadn't been all sunshine and unicorns. Some of her deepest issues hadn't come out until they'd said "I do," but they were working through those together in couples therapy. Kara continued to see her counselor on her own as well.

And she was making progress. The mere act of seeing Jeff didn't set her off like it once had. Maybe it helped that Warren went along for drop-offs in case Kara needed backup. Something about his presence had Jeff on his best behavior.

Small gift bag in hand, Rose skipped across the room and plopped it in Warren's lap. "Here you go."

"Thank you, Rosie-Posie."

Rose beamed at his nickname for her. "Can I help you open it?"

Warren glanced at Kara, who nodded. "Sure."

Kara's heart beat a bit harder in her chest. Would Warren be as excited as she had been?

Rose yanked at the tissue paper so hard that the present flew out and clattered onto the floor. She stooped and picked up the white stick, her nose wrinkling. "What is it?"

But Warren's head whipped toward her. "Is that what I think it is?"

A grin burst from Kara's lips. "If you think it's a positive pregnancy test, then yes. It is."

"Really?" His cheekbones lifted as he smiled and leaned forward, placing a hand tentatively on Kara's stomach. "We're having a baby?"

"A baby?" Rose pumped her fist in the air. "Yes, yes, yes!" Then she twirled around like a ballerina, spinning and spinning out her joy.

As for Warren, he leaned closer, pressing his forehead to Kara's. "I can't believe it."

"Are you … happy?"

"Are you kidding?" He kissed her softly. "This is amazing. A dream come true." Then he lifted his head and pointed to the mantel. "Rose, grab the bell. Quick."

Their daughter lifted up on her tiptoes and snatched Warren's grandfather's bell, then stepped through the crinkled tissue paper on the ground as she brought it over.

And together, Warren and Kara lifted it between them, ringing out the good news.

Quick Author's Note

Thank you so much for reading Kara and Warren's story! I loved writing this tale of healing and learning to love again.

Want to see our grumpy innkeeper Rebecca Trengrouse get her happily ever after? Check out *Like a Holiday Inn,* the next book in the Port Willis Romance series, where she is thrown for a loop when Ginny and Sarah's brother Benjamin shows up with an offer she most definitely wants to refuse…

Read on for a sneak peek...

If Rebecca Trengrouse could do one thing—and one thing only—for the rest of her life, it would be this.

This right here.

She sealed the plastic container of buttercream frosting she'd just whipped up and stepped back from the three layers of cake cooling on the counter. Inhaled the scent of sugar and vanilla in the air. Pictured how her hands would take what was in her head and physically make it reality in just three days.

Once she added the frosting and custom sugar decorations she'd been slaving over the last few weeks, the Donaldson wedding cake would be perfection.

Yes, perfection—something that could only be achieved in the kitchen.

A door creaked behind her. "Becs, it smells amazing in here!"

Rebecca tossed a glance over her shoulder at her friend Ginny Applegate, one eyebrow lifted. "Of course it does. This is a bakery." Ginny's bakery, to be exact—the one with the drool-worthy commercial oven her friend had graciously allowed Rebecca to use.

"Good point." Her brown ponytail bouncing, Ginny moved her lithe frame across the tiled floor to the white quartz island. "I'm so excited to see the finished product."

"I'm excited to make it happen." That's how she'd spend her time the day before the wedding, since the day of, Rebecca would be busy making sure the actual wedding went off without a problem.

Yes, she was cake baker, innkeeper, hostess, and wedding coordinator all in one pint-sized, one-woman show.

And she absolutely couldn't afford for everything not to go smashingly well.

After a slow autumn—and that loan she had stupidly taken out for kitchen renovations a year and a half ago at Rebecca's, her self-titled bed and breakfast in Port Willis, England—she needed the massive payday the wedding party would bring in.

Even if it meant the week of Christmas was completely bonkers.

Which was fine. It's not like Rebecca had any other plans. Dad wasn't in town anymore, after all. And Blake was up in London with his little family.

She was alone this Christmas.

Just the way she liked it.

And no, she wasn't in denial—thank you very much.

Ginny stuck her finger into the bowl Rebecca had used to mix the strawberry champagne frosting and placed it in her mouth, mmm-ing with pleasure. "When does the wedding party get here again?"

"The twentieth." Just two days from now. The wedding—which would be held in the B&B's backyard—wouldn't take place until December twenty-second, but the whole wedding party and their families would be descending on Rebecca's B&B in advance so they could settle in and enjoy their time together.

Ginny took another swipe of frosting. "I never thought you'd be able to top my mascarpone cream, but this is to die for. One point to you."

Rebecca allowed the corner of her mouth to upturn at the reminder of the friendly competition they had going. "As you Americans are so fond of saying, I had to bring my A game after I tasted your orange curd last week."

"Well, you most definitely did. Your bride is going to freak out over how amazing this is. Not to mention how beautiful it'll be once it's all put together." Ginny shook her slightly pink finger at Rebecca. "You've got talent, my friend. I still can't believe you never went to culinary school."

Rebecca blew her dishwater blonde bangs out of her face. "No need for school when you're raised with a spatula in your hand instead of a rattle."

Ginny snorted. "True. I had to sneak baking lessons from our cook because my parents didn't think it an acceptable pastime." The woman may have grown up in one of the wealthiest families in Boston, but you'd never know it to look at her with her casual jeans dusted with flour, zippered sweatshirt, and purple Converse sneakers. And even though they'd started out as enemies of a sort, even Rebecca hadn't been able to resist the charms of the bubbly American who made everyone her friend. "I'm jealous. I loved school but it was a beast."

"Well, you clearly made the most of it." Rebecca gestured around the kitchen. Five years ago, Ginny had opened Once Upon a Time Bakery after selling the bookstore next door to her best friend and fellow American, Sophia Rose. "Your bakery is more popular than Trengrouse Bakery ever was."

Ginny's face twisted into a grimace, just as it did anytime Rebecca's now-defunct family bakery was mentioned. "Becs—"

Rebecca carried her supplies to the large stainless-steel sink and started washing them, falling into the familiar routine. "Thanks again for letting me use your kitchen to bake the cake. Your oven is a dream."

"Anytime." Ginny sidled up to Rebecca. "Look, I

know you've forgiven me over what happened to your family's bakery, but—"

"There's nothing to forgive." After all, while Rebecca may have believed so initially, it wasn't Ginny's fault that Dad had decided to close up shop without even checking whether Rebecca wanted to continue the family legacy. He'd just assumed she didn't want it.

And why not? Rebecca had stayed away from Port Willis ever since leaving town at eighteen to attend college in Edinburgh. To her family—to Blake, Dad, and Mum, God rest her soul—it must have seemed like that.

They'd had no idea that coming back here to the small village on the Cornish coast, running the bakery, had been her dream since she'd been a little girl.

Now, her dream was just to survive. To not utterly drown in the blood-red financials of the B&B. If she could only keep on top of repaying that loan …

But it was fine. It would be fine. Landing the Donaldson wedding was just the sort of miracle she'd been praying for—well, not actually praying, since God seemed to have forgotten her too.

Regardless, the wedding would help her dig out of the hole in which she'd found herself. She'd get paid, and then she'd experience a reprieve.

Until the next bill came due.

But for now, it was something.

"I still feel bad."

Rebecca hip-checked Ginny. "That's because you're too nice. Just be a cheeky bird like me and choose not to care what anyone else thinks." She scrunched her nose and lifted her chin. "There's a reason everyone in town calls me the Ice Queen."

Laughing, Ginny shoved her hands into the soap bubbles and grabbed a dirty measuring bowl and scrub brush. "Aw, Becs, you forget I know your secret. You're secretly soft inside."

"You go ahead and keep thinking that. You're the only one who does." She glanced around the kitchen, sighed. "If I could hole away here forever and never interact with another soul—save you, maybe—I could die a happy woman."

After a beat of silence came Ginny's teasing reply. "For someone who dislikes the human population as much as you do, it's a bit ironic you purchased a bed and breakfast."

Rebecca shrugged. It had seemed like a good idea at the time. Because if she couldn't have her own bakery, at least she could cook and bake for an appreciative audience in some way.

It had also allowed her to stay in her hometown, take care of Dad in his old age.

Though that hadn't exactly worked out the way she'd imagined it, now had it?

"Why do you think I put the blasted thing up for

sale six months ago?" It had nothing to do with Dad's remarriage and move to Falmouth to be near Melanie's family.

None.

Okay, maybe a little. That, and the fact she was hardly keeping things afloat. And yet …

She plunged a mixing bowl into the suds and scrubbed. Hard.

Ginny paused, glanced sideways at Rebecca. "Still no offers?"

"No good ones." Everyone wanted to undercut her price—by a significant amount. It wasn't her fault the economy had taken a dip, that realty prices had fallen.

If she was going to divest herself of her livelihood, her home, then she was going to get a good price for it. Enough to start over.

To get a new dream.

Otherwise, her inheritance—the only thing her dad had ever given her—would be wasted. Gone.

With nothing to show for it.

"I don't understand how you haven't been able to find a buyer. Who wouldn't want to move to this gorgeous town?"

Now it was Rebecca's turn to snort. "It's tiny, for one. And sure, we have a few festivals like any small town, but as far as tourists go … well, the B&B sits below half capacity much of the time these days." Far below.

She lifted the clean mixing bowl out of the sink and snagged a towel to dry it.

"Surely you could find a way to drive more traffic in, yeah?" Ginny flipped her ponytail over her shoulder. "I know how you feel about marketing, but you're the only inn in town—"

"Don't you dare say that dirty M word to me, Ginny Rose." Rebecca shuddered at the thought of willingly putting her private affairs out there for the world to see. And yet, that was how most businesses worked, wasn't it?

It was official. She was, quite possibly, the worst businesswoman in England. Maybe in the whole world.

Ginny rolled her eyes, grinning. "Well, if you ever want some social media tips, or an updated website, you know Steven would be happy to help."

"Tell your delightful husband thanks, but no thanks."

"Alright, alright." Ginny held up her soapy hands in surrender. "But for the record, I hate the idea of you not living next door. I'll miss you so much whenever you go—though you know I'll do my best to convince you to stay in town even after you've sold."

Ginny was sweet, but her life had gotten so busy after the whirlwind adoption of their three kids—four-year-old Macy and seven-year-old twins Lila and Jessie—that she hadn't had as much time to knock about with Rebecca lately anyway.

Between Ginny, her sister Sarah, and Sophia, who had a handsome professor husband and three kids of her own, most of the thirty-something women in this tiny village were living the wife and mom life. Something Rebecca would never have.

Because getting married meant opening your life to someone, and for Rebecca, that had only ever led to a broken heart.

She was better on her own.

"There's nothing left for me here."

"Thanks a lot."

"You know what I mean."

"I know you mean your family left. But I consider you family, Becs."

Unshed tears scorched Rebecca's eyes. Oh, no way. She was not going to cry. Especially not in front of someone else. That wasn't Rebecca's style.

"And speaking of that, did you decide about Christmas Eve?" Ginny continued. "And of course Christmas Day too. Or are you getting together with your dad and stepmom? Will your brother be in town this year? I keep forgetting to ask if he decided to come down from London."

Ugh. Could she bury herself under a pile of muffins and just avoid the holidays altogether? "I don't know what Dad is doing." And maybe she would, if she'd answered his calls or listened to his voicemails. "As for Blake, you know we're more of the *I'll text you on holidays and for family emergencies but that's it* sibling variety."

Sometimes she wished…

But it didn't matter what she wished. This is what was. First, she'd left. Then, she'd returned—and everyone else had left *her*. Apparently, that's what Trengrouses did.

"I'll be fine on my own." Rebecca forced a tiny smile. "There will be a lot of cleanup after the wedding party leaves. Thanks for the invitation, though."

"Well, it stands." Her friend chewed her bottom lip, looked like she wanted to say more. Of course she did. She wanted everyone to be as happy as she was. She'd invite a peddler off the street if she thought he didn't have somewhere to go for Christmas. Why not the Ice Queen too?

But that's just who Ginny Applegate was. Why the woman bothered being Rebecca's friend at all was a complete and utter mystery.

Side by side, she and Ginny worked until all the dishes were clean. At one point, Charlotte—the twenty-something, quiet brunette who worked the front of the bakery most days—stuck her head in and asked Ginny to come answer a question about ingredients for a customer. Ginny dried her hands and scampered off.

Rebecca turned to examine the wedding cake

layers. Finding them completely cooled, she whipped up some simple syrup and brushed the layers with it to keep the cake moist. Then she wrapped them up and cleared a spot in Ginny's walk-in fridge for the cake. Her friend had much more space than she did and once again had showcased her generosity by allowing Rebecca to store the cake there.

Rebecca had worked up a bit of a sweat putting everything back where it belonged when she heard the door swing open. "I'm about done in here"—she glanced up—"oh."

Ginny had her sister with her. "Look who I found."

Though only slightly taller than Rebecca, confident redheaded Sarah Bentley-Hammett was the picture of poise—the complete opposite of Ginny in many ways, though they had the same smile. Like Ginny, Rebecca and Sarah hadn't gotten off on the best of feet, but they maintained a cordial acquaintance now. "Hey, Rebecca."

"Hullo."

"Need help with anything in here?" Sarah rubbed her hands together. "I'm on a break." She was an attorney and the president of the London branch of New Dawn Women's Council, a nonprofit that provided free legal aid to battered women. She and her photographer husband Michael had recently moved from Boston to Port Willis, his hometown, and she worked remotely—usually from Ginny's bakery—while he watched their toddler Judah at home in between photo shoots.

"You sure you aren't just avoiding a phone call from one of your donors?" Ginny teased.

"Ugh, fine. Yes." Sarah slumped against the counter. "He's such a complainer. I can't take it. My ears bleed every time I have to talk with him."

"Ooo, the old guy who thinks he's God's gift to all mankind?" Ginny threw her arm around her sister's shoulders. "Which is ridiculous, because we all know that's chocolate and peanut butter."

Sarah laughed. "That's the one."

A strange burning filled Rebecca's chest as she turned from their sisterly banter. She and Blake had never had that kind of relationship, though she was only a few years older. From what Ginny had said, she and Sarah—and their middle brother, who still lived in Boston and worked for one of their dad's many companies—hadn't been close until recently. The brother still had never visited Port Willis, but they talked via phone as much as he was able.

Sarah straightened. "I know I'm not a fabulous baker like either of you, but please save me from myself and give me a job."

"I'll leave that up to Ginny. I've gotta run." Rebecca eyed the four platters of brownies and muffins she and Ginny had made this morning before she'd baked the cake. Time to get those stored in the B&B's freezer for later this week. Wedding guests tended to snack often in between festivities, and she needed to be on the top of her game.

Because happy brides spread the word. And weddings paid a lot—they not only booked out the ten-room B&B to capacity, but they also used the grounds out back for the ceremony and usually hired Rebecca to cater or provide the cake.

Enough weddings, and maybe she'd pay off that stinking loan.

Maybe she didn't have to sell.

Though sometimes, the idea of letting go of the inn felt right too.

Perhaps that was merely the exhaustion talking.

"Here, let us help." Before Rebecca could protest, Ginny grabbed two platters and Sarah snagged another, leaving one for Rebecca.

"Alright." Rebecca picked up the remaining platter, catching a whiff of cocoa despite the plastic wrap covering the chocolate cherry muffins, and headed out the kitchen door into the front of the bakery filled with tittering customers. With pops of yellow, Ginny's place displayed all the bright character and charm of the woman herself, inviting with its modern yet comfortable aesthetic.

Trengrouse Bakery had had history.

But Once Upon a Time Bakery had heart. Rebecca wouldn't have wanted to compete with that even if her dad *had* left her the bakery instead of retiring and closing up shop.

A bearded man with gray-streaked brown hair and a long black trench coat opened the door as the women approached, letting in a boost of chill along with a three-legged dog.

"Oliver Lincoln!" Ginny exclaimed, her attention directed at the man. "I thought you guys weren't coming in for a few days."

"Aunt Mavis is having a minor procedure tomorrow and needed someone to cover the antique shop, so we came early."

"Oh, I hope she's okay," Sarah chimed in.

"Nothing to be concerned about. She'll be in and out the same day."

"I'm glad to hear that." Despite the platters of food, Ginny crouched next to the white dog and let him lick her cheek. "And Rascal! Oh, how I missed you. Where's your mama?"

"Joy's next door at the bookshop doing that jumping up and down thing she always does when first being reunited with Sophia." Oliver's eyes twinkled as they always did when speaking of his American—and very boisterous—wife.

It was rather disgusting, actually. The way all of these women had come across the pond and turned Rebecca's male British counterparts' brains to complete rubbish …

Fine, it was adorable, but Rebecca would never in

a million years admit it. "We've got to get these treats back to the B&B."

Oliver held out his free hand. "Can I assist you?"

"We've got it sorted."

He nodded and held the door wider so she could slip through. The other women expressed their gratitude.

Rebecca probably should as well. "Oliver?"

His eyebrow arched. "Yes?"

"If you're available, you and Joy are welcome to join us tomorrow night at the B&B."

Sarah and Ginny exclaimed their agreement over the Lincolns joining in for the caroling and dinner tradition they'd started last year. Oliver grinned. "We'll be there. Thanks, mates."

"Good." Without another word, Rebecca turned and trudged onward, not stopping to wait for Sarah and Ginny to follow. From their chatter, it sounded as if they might be another few minutes, but this platter was growing heavy.

The sun set early in December, and the moon cast a gentle glow on the cobblestone street and pavements lined with black iron lampposts. The pastels of the buildings themselves had been muted to darker tones, but even that couldn't dim the beauty of Rebecca's hometown. At the bottom of sloping High Street, the twinkling waters of the harbor reflected the stars, casting an ethereal kind of magic back into the air.

Oh, why had she spent so many years away from this place?

Rebecca breathed in the crisp air. It didn't snow much in Port Willis, and that was one thing she missed about Edinburgh—the only thing.

All the people, the crowds … Daniel—those things she never wanted to see again.

This place smacked of home.

And yet, she wasn't sure she really belonged.

Because if home was where your heart was, maybe she didn't belong anywhere. After all, half this town didn't think Rebecca Trengrouse *had* a heart. Or, at the very least, that it was iced over.

It didn't take long to reach the B&B's front door. Rebecca wrestled it open with one hand and propped it with a doorstop for Ginny and Sarah, who were still somewhere behind her.

Turning, she promptly gasped back a shriek at the sight of a man standing at the wooden reception desk. "Who … What?"

The man removed his beanie and ran a hand through his crop of thick brown hair. His dark chocolate eyes sparked with amusement. "Speechless in my presence, I see." His American accent grated against her ears. He peeled off his gloves and stuffed them into the pocket of his leather jacket—one that must have cost him more than a whole week's stay at her B&B. Did they actually make leather that fine? "Don't worry. I'm used to it."

Her brain took a moment to process what he was saying. "I'm sorry?"

"No need to apologize, Beautiful." And then, this stranger had the audacity to wink at her.

She got the sudden urge to take a muffin from this tray and shove it into his impeccably chiseled face. "You're daft if you think I was apologizing. I don't apologize. To anyone. Especially not an arrogant dolt like you."

Instead of scowling at her like Daniel used to when she'd turn to a rant, the man's grin widened. And something about *that* was even more irksome.

"And here I've heard so many wonderful things about Port Willis hospitality."

Wait, was he a guest? She didn't have any reservations last time she'd checked. Rebecca narrowed her eyes. "Who are you?"

"Benjamin?" A squeal erupted behind Rebecca as Ginny rushed inside, followed quickly by Sarah, whose bootheels clacked on the wood floors. Ginny dropped her platters on the top of the desk and flung herself into the man's arms.

Benjamin? This was Ginny and Sarah's brother from Boston? The one they'd sometimes described as a playboy and serial dater?

That definitely made sense.

Ginny released her brother's broad shoulders and turned to Sarah. "Did you know he was coming?"

"I'm just as surprised as you." With a gentle smile,

Sarah stepped into Benjamin's arms, then smacked the back of his head like the big sister she was. "You should have said something."

"I wanted to surprise my favorite sister."

Without asking which sister that would be, Sarah and Ginny looked at each other and rolled their eyes, as if used to their brother's antics.

Rebecca, however, did not have any familial obligation to stay in this room any longer than necessary and put up with this rubbish. Grabbing one of Ginny's trays along with her own, she high-tailed it to the kitchen and dropped them onto the gray quartz countertop. On her way back to take the other two trays, all three of the Bentley siblings turned her way.

Too bad she had already been spotted, else she'd have scooted back inside until they'd left.

Ginny put a hand on Benjamin's upper arm. "Benjamin, this is Becs—Rebecca Trengrouse. She's the owner. Becs, this is my older brother, Benjamin."

"We've met," he said. And there was that ridiculous grin again—the one that made her want to crawl out of her skin. Hit something.

"Yes. Most pleasurable moment of my life." Oh, how she hoped he could hear the sarcasm in her tone, though he'd have to be completely barmy not to. "Don't let me keep you. I'm sure you all want to get back to whoever's house Benjamin is staying at and get on with your family business."

Ginny opened and shut her mouth. Sarah winced.

Benjamin just stood there grinning at her like she was the Queen Consort inviting him to tea.

"What did I miss?" Rebecca's hand landed on a hip.

"Well …" Ginny tugged on her hair and separated the ends in that nervous way she had. "We only have the two bedrooms."

Yes, and all three girls were crammed into one of them with a bunk and another single twin bed.

Hold on. Was Ginny saying what Rebecca thought she was? "What about you?" she asked Sarah.

Sarah scrunched her nose. "Kara and Warren are staying with us. In fact"—she lifted her hand, checking her smart watch—"I need to head to the airport now to get them." She kissed Benjamin on the cheek. "Let's catch up tonight after dinner, okay? Come over around eight for dessert?"

"Sounds great."

Sarah rushed out. That only left Ginny, who still stood there looking like she'd snatched the last biscuit from the jar. She looked around the B&B—the dining room with a table for twelve, the sidebar where Rebecca set out food every morning, and beyond, to the cozy living room and fireplace lined with bookshelves. "You've got space here, don't you?"

Of course she did. At least until the wedding party arrived in two days.

But was the little bit of money she'd make from Benjamin's stay enough to make up for the fact that she'd have to spend the night under the same roof as this dodgy messer? Serve him breakfast? Put up with his arrogant mug?

"What about your couch?" she asked. "He could sleep there."

"Have you seen him?" Ginny hooked her thumb back at her brother, who bounced his gaze between the two women, mischief in his eyes. "Dude wouldn't fit."

What little mind Rebecca had for finances warred with her emotions. "Well, you're going to have to suss it out, because I don't have space."

"Really, Becs?"

Ooo, was that an edge of annoyance in Ginny's voice? Ginny, who had probably never said a cross word to anyone in her life? Who, in truth, put up with more of Rebecca's foul moods than anyone else ever had without complaint?

Rebecca pinched the bridge of her nose between her thumb and forefinger. "Fine. He can stay. Only two nights, though. I won't have room as of the twentieth."

Ginny's smile took up her whole face and her embrace nearly smothered Rebecca. "Thank you!

We'll figure something out for the rest of the time. Right, bro?" She looked back at Benjamin.

"Sure we will."

"Great. I've got to get back to the bakery." She pointed at her brother and then to Rebecca. "You two play nice." Then she was gone.

"I'll be nice. Perfectly nice." Benjamin stroked his stubbled jaw and winked at Rebecca. "Maybe by the time I have to leave, you won't want me to go." Then he reached into his pocket, pulled out his wallet, and held out his credit card to Rebecca.

She rounded the desk, yanked the card from his grip, stuck it in the card reader, and leaned forward to meet his overconfidence head-on. "And maybe a blizzard will hit Port Willis." Ha. If they even got a small dusting of snow each year—especially at Christmastime—they'd be lucky. Any significant snow the meteorologists ever forecasted always seemed to skip right over their little village.

The printer whirred as it printed his receipt. She snagged it and handed it to him, along with a biro.

He slanted closer as he took the ballpoint pen. "So you're saying it's a possibility then?"

Well, technically there had been that blizzard in 1891 that was famous in these parts. But that had been a freak storm. Never likely to be repeated again.

"Possible only if I fall and whack my head and forget I have a brain. Sure. There's a chance."

If she'd thought Benjamin's smile had been bright before, what he shot her now had her eyes burning. "A chance is all I need."

Come fall in love with Rebecca, Benjamin, and the entire village of Port Willis in Like a Holiday Inn, Book 4 in the Port Willis Romance series, available today on your favorite ebook platform.

OR

Save yourself a little money by picking up Port Willis: The Complete Collection box set, which includes all four Port Willis sweet romance novellas.

BOOKS BY LINDSAY HARREL

The Barefoot Sisterhood Series

The Inn at Walker Beach

Walker Beach Series

All At Once (exclusively available in the Walker Beach
box set)

All of You, Always

All Because of You

All I've Waited For

All You Need Is Love

Port Willis Series

The Secrets of Paper and Ink

Like a Winter Snow

Like a Christmas Dream

Like a Silver Bell

Like a Holiday Inn

Standalones

The Joy of Falling

The Heart Between Us

One More Song to Sing

Lindsay Harrel is a lifelong book nerd who lives in Arizona with her young family and two golden retrievers in serious need of training. When she's not writing or chasing after her children, Lindsay enjoys making a fool of herself at Zumba, curling up with anything by Jane Austen, and savoring sour candy one piece at a time.

She also writes sweet romantic comedies (same sweetness, same heat level!) under the pen name Kristin Canary. Check out her books there at kristincanary.com.

www.ingramcontent.com/pod-product-compliance
Lightning Source LLC
Chambersburg PA
CBHW061533310726

48972CB00008B/2438